SECRETS IN BAR HARBOR

MOUNT DESERT ISLAND SERIES

KATIE WINTERS

ALL RIGHTS RESERVED. No part of this publication may be reproduced, distributed, or transmitted in any form or by any means, including photocopying, recording, or other electronic or mechanical methods, without the prior written permission of the publisher.

Copyright © 2021 by Katie Winters

This is a work of fiction. Any resemblance of characters to actual persons, living or dead is purely coincidental. Katie Winters holds exclusive rights to this work. Unauthorized duplication is prohibited.

PROLOGUE

Six Months Ago

THE TEMPTATION TO breathe was overwhelming, and yet I knew if I gave in, it would be my end. I frantically searched the liquid blue depths for Max as my lungs burned. He was there, somewhere. He had to be—I felt him.

"Max! I heard you call. I'm here."

Suddenly the water was gone. There was darkness, a harsh light, and then that horrible sound— shovels of gritty, wet dirt, falling into a deep, dark hole within the earth.

Although I knew better than to do it, I peeked into the abyss. I still felt Max out there somewhere— floating between this realm and the next. But there, in the center of the dark hole, lay an empty casket. The black-as-night soil cascaded over the wood polished shell, where a body should have lay. The casket would remain empty, a symbol of my pain.

This casket was meant to be Max's final resting place. It was meant to cocoon my forever soulmate, the only man I'd ever loved.

But as I gazed down, still more shovels of soil crashed across the space where his body should have been. The light he'd brought to the world had been extinguished forever.

I felt the truth of what I'd always known: his body would never be found.

Heather's mind fought sleep paralysis. She ached to be with Max, floating like a spineless jellyfish through the waves. Max had been an oceanographer, a lover of those mad depths of curiosity and danger. Only in her dreams did Heather have such bravery. Her psyche was on an urgent quest to find him again.

The dreams were Heather's only relief. Even now, as she edged out of this one and into the harsh realm of the living, she fought to remain. It was the closest she ever got to her husband. She had no life of her own, not out there.

But the external world had a mind of its own. Now, a metallic shriek pulsed. The sound penetrated her ears, sharp as needles.

Disoriented, she grunted. "Shut up!" With each stab of the alarm, she felt yanked away from her hungry search for her love. The sound ignored her cries, and she kicked the comforter in anger as her stomach lurched. The thick blanket trapped her legs, holding her in its tentacles but denying her the dream. Sweat billowed across her back and across her cheeks as the sound grew louder. In desperation, she rolled from the bed and landed on the hand-knotted Turkish rug with a thump.

Where did the sound come from? Frustrated, Heather grabbed the black Maglite from her nightstand, her weapon of choice and began stalking the piercing shrieks. From one room to the next, the sound bounced off the plaster walls as it hid from her, just as Max always did in her dreams. Finally, there it was— the culprit of that annoying sound that pulled her from her reverie—a smoke alarm with failing batteries. It was too high to reach, so she did what any sensible person would do. She swung the flashlight over her head, smashing the alien device. At least it was quiet in death.

Back in the bedroom, she flipped on the light switch and dragged her vanity chair against the tall wardrobe. She clambered atop the chair, placed a hand on the wardrobe knob for balance while she searched up top. "Ah," she sighed with pleasure as she gripped the small box. She then clambered back down, kicked aside the comforter, and slid down the side of the bed until she sat straight-legged on the rug.

Max had always smoked Marlboro Reds. This was a box she'd found during the days after the accident out at sea when the ocean liner had exploded off the coast of Nova Scotia. It remained heavy: seventeen cigarettes still within the box of twenty. She wiped aside a tear with the sleeve of her sleepshirt, then slowly opened the lid of the box and held it to her nostrils. With closed eyes, Heather hesitantly drew in the tobacco scent. If she blanked her mind, just so, just for one second, she could still believe Max was there, lying next to her, a sheen coat of sweat making his tanned body slick after their lovemaking. Oh, how she'd worshipped those moments. Max, the triumphant male. Her powerful source of strength and knowledge and unconditional love.

Sometimes, when the pain was just too much, she would remove one of the cigarettes and put it between her lips. The bitter taste coated her tongue—just as it had when he'd kissed her.

Sometimes, pain was a comfort when the alternative was a void.

With cautious fingers, she slid the cigarette back into its casket and then put it back atop the wardrobe. If she were careful and kept them dry, perhaps their scent would hold her for the fifty years she and Max had planned to be each other's soulmates.

She could only wish.

CHAPTER ONE

BEEP. BEEP. BEEP.

Heather Harvey Talbot's alarm seemed to blare out from another realm. Slowly, her eyes peeled back as she inhaled sharply. Her skin was clammy and thick with sweat. She swung a wayward arm off to the right, grabbed her phone, and turned off her alarm as her psyche crawled back to reality.

She'd had the dream again. It had always been the same dream since the accident, nearly a year before. A dream she couldn't escape.

She drew her knees up, placed her back against the bed frame, and splayed her hands over her face, which was just as damp as the rest of her body. Max's funeral. Gosh. What had gotten into her? Why did her brain want to fight her so much?

She was endlessly disconcerted. What day was it? Maybe sometime in August or September? She wore flannel pajamas, and all the windows were latched shut, but something within her knew, intuitively, that it wasn't yet winter. In Portland, Maine, when winter hit, it was a frigid cold that you couldn't forget.

Heather gripped her phone again and tapped at the screen to brighten it. It was seven-thirty in the morning. Her girls, Bella and Kristine, both lived in New York City and had apparently sent her a number of texts long after Heather had gone to bed.

BELLA: Mom? Are you okay? We got your message...

KRISTINE: Mom— do you need us to come home? Please, tell us if you need us. We'll be there ASAP.

Heather couldn't remember having dialed her daughters. She inspected her call history and found that, sure enough, she'd called them seven times— four times to Bella and three times to Kristine. She had then left a voicemail on Kristine's phone. She had no memory of that. This frightened her but in a vague sense.

Heather padded down to the kitchen through the grey light of the morning. The calendar on the wall read: August, and someone — maybe her, had put large black X marks through all the dates up till August 28th. It was a Tuesday, somehow, a rainy, grey, dismal Tuesday.

It was never up to her when the dreams reared their ugly heads. She siphoned off the coffee grounds into the filter and propped it up in the coffee maker. In a moment, the maker began to perform its glug-glug action, and she placed her elbows on the counter and re-read the messages from her daughters.

She knew she needed to call them. Probably, both were already awake; such was the magic of being twenty-two. You could go to bed at two in the morning and rise at six, ready to conquer a brand-new day. It had been a long time since Heather's body had managed that.

Before she could rally herself to call, Kristine's face popped up on the screen. Heather's eyes clamped shut with worry.

Maybe it was finally time to tell them about her recurring nightmare— about the ocean and empty casket and her endless quest to find him.

Since his body had never been found, they'd held a closed casket funeral as an attempt to find closure. That closure had never come for Heather.

Maybe dreaming was her mind's way of rectifying a horrific situation. It was her mind's way of mourning. But when she awoke in the silence of the morning, without Max by her side, she felt on the verge of a nervous breakdown. She knew she had to hold it together, if not for herself, for her daughters.

"Hi, honey." She was proud of how bright and cheery she sounded.

"Mom?" Kristine's voice wavered. "Are you okay?"

"I'm just fine," Heather affirmed. She turned, gripped the coffee pot, and poured herself a heaping cup, which resulted in droplets of coffee across the counter. Why couldn't she control herself?

"You called Bella and me so many times last night," Kristine returned. "And that voicemail..."

Heather winced. There was no way to know what she had said. She glanced toward the far window, with its view out across Casco Bay, which now looked grey and foreboding in the early, somber light. Alongside the window sat a glass of half-drunk wine, along with a near-empty bottle. Clearly, Heather had really gone for it, lonely-widow-style. And she had wanted her daughters along for the ride, as well.

"You said something about going to Bar Harbor of all places," Kristine demanded now. "Renting out the house in Portland and going back to those people you always said never mattered to us?"

Right. There it was: a stab of memory.

Just yesterday, she had told one of her older sisters, Nicole, that she would come to stay with her in Bar Harbor for a while. It had been a surprise, in and of itself, that Nicole was there at all, especially after their promise to never contact the Keating family.

But the way Nicole had described Bar Harbor? It had beckoned to her. It had felt like a respite from the endless loneliness, which had begun to feel like a dark cloud over everything else. The weight of it had grown too powerful. And wine? Well. It had been her only solace for too long.

Max had been gone for over a year. It was time to stop digging herself into this reckless hole of sorrow. The term for it wasn't "move on," because how could she ever move on without him? Max was the love of her life. His disappearance into the dark depths of the ocean had ripped her in two. She would spend the rest of her days a shell of her previous self.

"I told your Aunt Nicole I would come see her for a while," Heather finally rasped. "You know, she's been through so much." This was true, in a way, but also not.

"Hmm." Kristine sounded doubtful. Both daughters were entirely too smart for their own good. They could see through anything. "I just don't understand any of this. Why did Aunt Nicole go back to Bar Harbor, anyway?"

Heather was silent for a moment. She was too numb to be angry with Nicole the way her older sister, Casey, was. She was fiery with animosity.

"I can't explain it, Kristine," Heather finally told her. "But Nicole probably needed a break after her divorce. And my Uncle Joseph just died in Bar Harbor and, well..."

"Yes. The Uncle Joe you never knew," Kristine pointed out.

Heather paused. Her teeth nibbled against her lower lip. There was still so much she didn't understand about her sister's trek to Bar Harbor— stuff she'd only grasp upon her arrival.

"I just need to get out of here, Kristine," Heather breathed finally. "I can't be in this house, with all its memories. Not right now. I have nightmares almost every night."

Kristine was quiet for a long time. In the background, her speakers blared sounds of the radio.

"Bella and I can really come home if you want us to, Mom," Kristine finally offered. "Or we've talked about moving you here to the city. It's not like you can't afford it."

Heather had been to the city to visit her daughters several times, but only once since Max's disappearance. The chaos of the city, the rush of the pedestrians, the smells and the sounds— it all had overwhelmed Heather to such a degree that she'd had an anxiety attack and spent much of the afternoon strewn across Bella's bed. They'd canceled their dinner reservations and ordered food in, which Heather had hardly touched. By then, she had lost a good twenty pounds since Max's accident, whittling herself away to nearly nothing.

Since then, she had put some weight back on and settled into some sort of schedule for herself. But she hadn't made it back to the city; instead, she'd paid for her daughters to fly back every few months, picked them up from the airport, and tried her best to perform all the duties of a mentally healthy mother, even as their father remained lost at sea.

"I just wish we could help you," Kristine said somberly. "But our jobs are here and..."

"Don't worry about it. I've already packed up everything I'm taking with me. Heading over to your Aunt Casey's this morning for breakfast, and then I'll be on my way."

"I'm sure Aunt Casey has a few things to say about this trip," Kristine said doubtfully.

Heather chuckled. It was true that her eldest sister, Casey, was never one to mince words.

"I'm sorry to worry you," Heather offered finally. "I have to run. But I'll call you when I get to Bar Harbor. Okay?"

Kristine grumbled. "Fine, I'm off to work, but Mom?"

Heather's heart pattered wildly. "What is it, honey?"

"I love you. Bella does, too." She paused for a moment and then added, "That voicemail really scared us. Please, just keep us in the loop. We can be there in a heartbeat if you'll just ask us to be."

When Kristine and Heather hung up, Heather took a sip of her coffee and watched as the clouds continued to roll over Portland, formidable, a constant reminder that summer was now on its way out, replaced soon with dark autumn days and sinister winters. She hardly remembered the previous winter. She had spent most of it curled up in a ball, hiding from calls from her editor and publisher, praying for some kind of miracle. Perhaps time would bring Max back to her, she'd thought. Perhaps if she just waited it out.

But Max wasn't coming back. Who was she kidding? There was no hope.

And she couldn't remain in this house any longer. She would go insane if she did. Her nightmares were proof that she was halfway there already.

CHAPTER TWO

"IT'S IDIOTIC, is what it is." Casey's bright red robe whipped out on either side of her as she stormed through the kitchen. She looked like a regal queen; her chin lifted and her eyes violent with rage. "She kept it from us that she went there, and now? Now she's all 'woe is me, I have to run the whole restaurant and inn by myself.' Jesus, Heather. We made a pact, didn't we? Never to involve ourselves with that side of the family!"

Casey glared down at Heather, who sat at her kitchen island with her legs dangling down from the stool. She had hardly touched her eggs and sausage and biscuit and had spent the majority of Casey's rant moving little pieces of egg around her plate.

"Speak of the devil." Casey stabbed her phone and called out, "Nicole? You're on speaker. I have Heather here, and we both think you've lost your mind."

Heather cleared her throat. "For the record, I think we're all a little nuts."

Casey rolled her eyes as Nicole interjected.

"Casey, as usual, you've totally blown everything out of proportion," Nicole tried to stand her ground. "I think there's a lot to uncover about this place—a lot to discover. This restaurant, this inn— I mean, the location is spectacular. Now that Uncle Joe is..." She trailed off.

"He died, Nicole. You can say it." Casey shot out as her nostrils flared. "We don't have to mince words."

Nicole had been guarded about her time in Bar Harbor thus far. Heather had a strange hunch that she and their Uncle Joe had become close during his last months of life. Probably, due to their past, she was a bit hesitant to tell her other sisters this.

"Well, anyway. The restaurant and inn belong to us," Nicole affirmed. "And you'd be silly not to see it, Case."

Casey arched an eyebrow toward Heather. In a low tone, she replied, "You know I'm here for you if you need anything. You don't have to go to Bar Harbor on some kind of quest to find yourself."

"You know I can hear you, right?" Nicole blared on the other end.

Heather's cheeks burned. Again, she slid a bit of egg off to the right. "It's not about you, Casey. It's not even about Uncle Joe. I'm just curious about— about our past, about our father. I can't explain why."

This annoyed Casey all the more. "You know he left us. And then he died by suicide. I mean, the guy has been gone for decades. Why now, Heather?"

Heather shrugged and took a sip of her coffee. How could she explain to Casey that her insides felt so hollowed out? She was willing to put anything in there, fill herself with facts and stories, so as not to fixate on the true horror of her life: that her husband had died at sea, along with many of his crew.

"I just don't know why you're not the least bit curious," Nicole shot over the speaker. "I mean, Uncle Joe and Dad left this beautiful place and the grounds to us— me and you two and our cousin, Uncle Joe's daughter, Brittany. Brittany wants nothing to do with any of it, mind you— and it's all ours, once her share is paid in full."

"Oh, great. A whole third of a property I don't want," Casey grumbled.

"You're ridiculous. You know that?" Nicole chided.

Heather sniffed as the normal chorus of Nicole and Casey's fight spun through her ears. They were a bit older than she was and a bit more similar, which allowed them to pick and prod each other until the other one snapped. Really, their stubbornness was their most powerful trait.

"Come on, Nicole. Tell us. Did you get all chummy with Uncle Joe? Did you discover family secrets that should make us run off and make peace with these people again?" Casey demanded. "Because it seems to me that everything you've done so far goes against the world we built here together in Portland. And I don't know what to make of it. It feels like you turned your back on us. And what are Heather and me to you, huh? We're your real family. It's us three against the world. You should know that."

Nicole was quiet for a long time. Heather's mind spun with worry. Finally, she stood so that her stool creaked beneath her.

"You haven't even touched your breakfast," Casey blared.

"Casey, please. I'm going to experience this place whether you like it or not. Nobody is going to force you to go," Heather said softly.

Casey's eyes dropped to the floor. Heather could practically feel the guilt upon both Casey and Nicole's shoulders. Neither had known what to do in the wake of Max's death.

"Okay. Sure. But don't come running to me when they disappoint you," Casey muttered as she closed her robe again and headed down the hallway, leaving Nicole still on speaker and Heather with her breakfast.

"Heather? You still there?" Nicole finally asked.

"Sure am."

"You're headed here today, right?"

"Yes, you can expect me," Heather affirmed. "I'll give you a call when I'm close. I can't wait to get out of Portland, Nic. It feels like my head is about to explode."

"I'll see you soon, sis. You're going to love it here."

THE DRIVE from Portland to Bar Harbor took approximately two hours and forty-five minutes. The grey smog of the early morning filtered into the mid-afternoon as Heather snaked her little Prius up along 295, north through Augusta, before dropping down into Mount Desert Island, where Bar Harbor was located on the eastern-most side, along Frenchman Bay.

Heather hadn't been to Bar Harbor more than a handful of times in her life, and always, she was a bit taken aback by the beauty of the place. Brightly colored buildings bunched up against a gorgeous harbor while wild green mountains swept upward into the Acadia National Park. Up above, Cadillac Mountain towered, with glorious views of Bar Harbor, the Cranberry Islands, and the Porcupine Islands from the many trails that snaked through every which way.

When she and Max had come here during the early era of their relationship, Max had taken her on a wild expedition through the woods. It had been the time before Heather had sold her first book, before Max had become a full-fledged oceanographer, and before the twins had been born. They had stood at the crest of Cadillac Mountain and gazed out at the immensity of the ocean and the glowing lines of sandy beaches, the last line of defense before the thick darkness of Frenchman Bay. At that moment, something about the ocean had frightened Heather. She'd gripped Max's hand hard and breathed, *"What is it about the ocean? Why do you have to be so involved in it? Can't you just enjoy it from here?"*

Max had held her hand with firm, powerful fingers. He'd known better than to belittle her fears. "It's silly, isn't it? But I thrive in these adventurous settings. I know I can only be a good husband, and someday, I hope, a good father if I listen to all these other parts of myself— my adventurous spirit, my hope to find the unknown. And Heather, I hope you, too, listen to your inner instincts. I hope you finally write the books you've tossed around your head for ages. I hope you don't have any kind of fear because, you know, I'm always here for you." He had splayed his hand across her cheek and stepped closer to her so that his breath was hot on her lips. How he'd challenged her! How marvelous it was to be seen, truly seen, so far above the shimmering ocean and the quaint little town below.

It had been them against the entire world.

But now, Heather drove her car through the outskirts of Bar

Harbor, then drove into a gas station to do another map-check on her phone. The restaurant and inn were located along the water, south of town, not far from where the mountains burst into the sky above and quite close to Thunder Hole and Sand Beach. Heather had a small laugh about a beach called Sand Beach; *was Water Beach taken?*

Heather turned on her GPS and drove the rest of the way to the inn as an annoying British woman spat directions to her, taking her down Park Loop Road toward the Keating Inn and Acadia Eatery—a large beautiful colonial white mansion with a wrap-around porch, beautiful glowing windows with black shutters that seemed to fight the dismal nature of the grey day, four stories, including a pointed attic space, which Nicole had said held a little unique library, where guests often sat to read and gaze out the window at Frenchman Bay just beyond. According to the website, which Heather had read over and over again as she'd made the decision to come, the Keating Inn and Acadia Eatery was a luxury hotel space, positioned on four gorgeous acres along the coast, with a near-perfect view of the sunrise, top-rated mattresses and appliances, and the kind of cuisine that made New England famous, with beautiful clam chowders, lobster, freshly-caught seafood from a local vendor, and to-die-for desserts. Just from the description alone, Heather's heart ached to go to the little hotel.

But now that she parked in the little lot alongside it, her spine quivered with apprehension. It was true what Casey said: they'd promised each other they would stay away from this side of the family. Their father had abandoned them, and in their eyes, the link to this family had faded at that moment. They hadn't needed it all this time. What had changed?

Well, that was easy. Everything had changed the minute Max had jumped onto that boat, never to be seen again. Heather now felt like a plane without a pilot, tossing herself into the turbulence of whatever happened next.

Just before she leaped out of the car, she sifted through her purse to find the little envelope in which she'd placed Max's leftover Marlboro Reds. She fought the urge to bring them to her nose. She couldn't give into their allure every time she felt off-kilter. Still, she hadn't been able to leave them at home on the wardrobe, not with another family staying there over the next few weeks. She had to have Max close by.

She stood in the slight spit of rain alongside her car. Although the drive hadn't been long, she'd again forgotten to feed herself, and her knees clacked together. Above her, the Keating Inn towered; its windows made her think of large eyes peering out of a big head. It seemed to watch her as she peered right back at it. An older couple, both with white hair and in dark green raincoats, walked along the edge of the porch and then gripped the railing; toward the far end of the porch, a young boy lifted a soccer ball into the air and then cast it out toward the back of the garden. On the third floor, a lightbulb flickered, then went out. Heather had the sense that a million little lives whipped in and out of this Keating Inn; that it was a safe haven for countless conversations and whispered secrets.

Perhaps here, in a space her father had once owned, in a world her father had once loved, she would find a piece of herself. Perhaps here, she would find a way to heal.

Or then again, she might only find a direct reflection of her own depression. After all, her father had taken his own life. Heather had never considered this route. She loved her daughters too much to ever abandon them like that. Still, she knew the darkness that existed in the early morning when she awoke and marveled that she had to keep going, even when it seemed unlikely she would find anything to live for.

"Is that my baby sister?" Nicole appeared on the wrap-around porch in a beautiful trench coat, which fluttered out on either side of her oval frame. Her brunette hair was thick, lush and vibrant; her smile was bright and just as inviting as ever. It occurred to Heather that Nicole should have been involved in hospitality all this time, rather than working in marketing, as she had for years. Her presence was something you craved.

Nicole took the steps one at a time, gripping the railing with a bright white hand as she made her way toward the parking lot. When she reached Heather, she flung her arms around her and placed her chin on Heather's shoulder.

"I've missed you so much," Nicole breathed.

Heather had felt such a distance between herself and every single other person in her life. She had felt like a nuisance to her daughters; she'd felt like a fool in Casey's kitchen, trying to explain why she wanted to go away. But here, in Nicole's arms, she felt suddenly safe, alive, and wanted. When their hug broke, she blinked back tears and nodded toward the inn above.

"I can't believe we own this place," she breathed. "It's magical in every way possible."

Nicole clapped her hands together and lifted up on her toes. "So glad to hear you say that. I worried Casey would taint your vision of this place."

Heather opened the trunk of her car and pulled out her suitcase. Nicole took it without question and beckoned for Heather to follow her up the staircase, back up toward the porch. Heather's tongue felt numb; her thoughts receded into the back of her mind. Their only task was to take the ten steps up to the porch, where Nicole finally dropped the suitcase near the door and waved toward a woman at the front desk.

"This is Jackie," Nicole explained as she allowed herself a final gasp post-staircase. "She's worked here forever."

Jackie was a redhead with a big gap between her front teeth. She might have been around fifty-five years old, ten years Heather's senior, but she had a girlish presence to her that made Heather smile. She yanked open the door and whispered, "Gosh, I just don't even know what to say. I am so sorry for your loss, Heather."

Right. Uncle Joseph. One of the reasons she'd come was to attend the funeral.

Jackie flung her arms around her, and Heather allowed herself, yet again, to be hugged. When the hug broke, Heather nodded and said, "It's really a sad thing." She wondered if Jackie believed her at all.

"Well, Nicole says she has a room all ready for you at the Keating House on the edge of the property," she told Heather. "It's a beautiful view of the bay." Jackie then gestured for one of the bellboys to take Heather's suitcase.

Heather returned her gaze to Nicole, curious about Nicole's previous months here. She seemed a perfect part of the patchwork, as though she'd slipped in without pause and just allowed herself the beauty of this world, of the people in it. Why had she given up on their promise? Where did she find all that forgiveness? Could Heather find it within herself?

"Would you like to see the library before we head over to the house?" Nicole asked.

Heather followed Nicole up the grand staircase to the attic floor, a tiny, white-washed room, with its view of the bay and another side window, with an iconic image of Cadillac Mountain. The room was lined with shelves and shelves of books, books from all genres and in several different languages, including French, German, Italian, and Japanese. Several couches were plump, in expectation of readers from all walks of life, hungry for a bit of quiet in the bright light of this upper floor.

"It's beautiful," Heather whispered, taking in every inch of the room.

Nicole stepped toward one of the further shelves and dropped to a crouch. "This is the children's section. Uncle Joe had a few of your books here for the kids. Look." Nicole removed three of the illustrated children's books, all of which Heather had written in her late twenties when her own babies had been bright and shining vessels of hungry curiosity. She'd dedicated all three books to Bella and Kristine. Now, seeing these books here in the midst of a world she'd long ago pledged never to come to, she was struck with how strange everything really was.

"I hope you'll be happy here," Nicole said. Her voice was tentative, filled with doubt. "When you said you wanted to come, I have to admit, I was surprised."

Heather lifted her eyes toward Nicole's. When Max had disappeared, both Nicole and Casey had tried to stay with Heather for days at a time, but Heather had resisted their advances and bid them on their way— telling them she needed her space. "I just don't want to worry about what I'm supposed to feed you guys for dinner! Just let me sleep!" she'd cried out to them once in frustration. Soon afterward, the sisters had decided they had created more stress than they'd wanted to and eased out of her life, one-by-one. Heather had been too proud, at that moment, to call them back, even though she'd known she needed them. Her stubbornness hadn't allowed her to.

The little wrinkle between Nicole's eyebrows grew deeper. "I know it's been really difficult for you, Heather. And I know you don't want to talk about it. But I'm here."

Heather's throat grew tight. She lifted her chin, still too proud to verbalize the density of her trauma. She had a million questions for Nicole, too. The tension between them was fraught.

"With all we've lost over these years," she began suddenly, "It got me thinking about Dad. About how much we never really knew about him."

Nicole nodded somberly. "I think he was a very complicated man."

Heather drew a little strand of hair behind her ear. "I wish I could have spoken to Uncle Joe about him before he died."

"He didn't love talking about our dad, either," Nicole admitted. "A few stories here and there, but generally, I think it was too painful. They worked together all those years and then, well. You know."

They held one another's gaze for a moment. Heather could half-imagine Nicole saying something here about Heather's depression and linking it with their father's mental health. Probably, Nicole was just grateful to keep an eye on Heather the way her daughters wanted to. The way Casey wanted to. All in all,

Heather knew it was just all of them being overprotective, and she couldn't fault any of them for it.

"Uncle Joe mentioned that he had some of Dad's things in the basement," Nicole offered then. "I haven't found the time to dig through any of it since I run myself ragged here at the inn and Eatery every day. But maybe, if you don't have too much writing to do..."

Heather longed to scoff at that. Writing? She hadn't written in months. That was what a younger, less-depressed version of Heather did— the successful Heather. The one who'd had endless love and a spitfire personality.

"I think I'll find the time," Heather admitted quietly.

Nicole shifted toward the door. "I'll let you get settled in. The funeral is tomorrow morning at eleven. You still up for it?"

Heather nodded and then shivered with the memory of Max's funeral, that empty casket, which now haunted her dreams.

Nicole knocked her fist against the doorframe. Downstairs, another group of tourists entered; a chorus of their voices drifted through the air, describing just how beautiful the area was.

"Nicole?" Heather tried.

Nicole's eyes danced back to find hers. "Yes."

"Thank you for suggesting this time in Bar Harbor. I really needed to get away."

Nicole nodded. "You know I'd do anything for you. Always have. Always will. We're family, and between you, me, and Casey, that means something a little different. Now -- let's head over to the main house, shall we? I stayed there for months with Uncle Joseph, but it's felt so empty since he died. I'll be so glad to have you there."

Heather padded down the staircase after Nicole as her thoughts ran amok. Here, in a beautiful mansion, upon acres of glorious grounds that went from Frenchman Bay up toward the mountains, there was so much at stake: family deaths, family secrets, and a funeral, to boot. After months and months of lackluster nothingness back in Portland, Heather felt her life was on the brink of something else again. It terrified her, but she knew it was the only way through this terror of darkness she had been living.

CHAPTER THREE

HEATHER TRIED NOT to allow Uncle Joe's funeral to drudge up the memories of Max's. Bar Harbor residents lined up at the funeral home, all in black dresses, dark suits, their voices low and their necks bowed with respect. The sight of them threatened to squeeze her heart till it stopped. She held her breath as long as she could as a way to distract herself, but it only reminded her of the nightmares— miles of ocean and lungs heavy with carbon dioxide.

Nicole stuffed a hand into her purse, gripped a Kleenex, and dabbed it against her nose. Heather arched an eyebrow with intrigue. Was Nicole crying? Had she actually gotten close enough to their uncle in the span of only a few months to feel such an immense loss?

"There she is." A woman in her forties sauntered up in dark heels and spread her arms out toward Nicole. Nicole fell into her embrace and exhaled deeply.

"He was such a good man, Brittany," Nicole whispered. "He really was."

Brittany. So this was their cousin, Uncle Joseph's only daughter. Nicole stepped back from their intimate embrace and gestured toward Heather. "This is my sister, Heather. She just arrived yesterday from Portland."

Heather then witnessed the slight shift in Brittany's eyes— proof that Brittany knew all about Heather, about Max's death, about her seemingly endless parade of depression. People couldn't help their pity; Heather knew this all too well. Still, it annoyed her that this woman, whom she had never met, already had this immense opinion of her and her tragedy.

"Heather. Thank you so much for coming to my father's funeral," Brittany whispered. She twitched as though she wanted to go in for a hug but couldn't sense if it was welcomed or not. "And welcome to Bar Harbor. There's— gosh, there's so much to say. You know, I've heard so much about you over the years. Uncle Joe always said it was perfect you were a writer. Just like your father always wanted to be. Like you fulfilled something Uncle Adam could never achieve for himself."

Heather's lips parted in shock at her words. *A writer, like her father?* Nobody had ever told her this. Goosebumps ran across her skin.

Funeral-goers had begun to drop into the many lines of overly-cushioned seats in preparation for the service. Brittany's voice faltered. "I have to find my kids and husband," she explained. "Good to meet you, Heather. Nicole. I'll see you afterward, I'm sure."

Heather and Nicole found seats in the middle. Heather felt she stuck out like a sore thumb— one of the nieces of the dead man before them, one of the ones who'd never called. At forty-four, wasn't she too old for such petty fights?

"What did Brittany mean about Dad being a writer?" Heather whispered.

"Shh," Nicole returned.

The man who approached the podium cleared his throat and introduced himself as the pastor of Uncle Joe's church. He was soft-spoken and seemingly kind, and his eyes watered as he spoke about Joe, as though they'd had a real friendship.

"To say that we all knew and loved Joe is an understatement of the century," the preacher began. "Joe was more than just a resident of the Bar Harbor community. He was a loyal friend, an honorable father, a wicked joke-teller and a beautiful woodworker. He was always there when you needed him, whether you needed your driveway shoveled of snow or your roof patched up or a place to stay for the night. Joe was always there."

Something strange and hard curved at the base of Heather's stomach. Who was this person this preacher described? Could this actually be her father's brother, her Uncle Joe— a man she, Casey, and Nicole had sworn to avoid for all these years? Sweat bubbled up on the back of her neck. Was this what regret felt like?

She suddenly felt that she'd missed so much.

Heather rolled her shoulders back and slipped her fingers tightly together. Off to the left, her cousin, Brittany, dabbed her cheek as tears rolled from her eye. Her children sat on either side of her, all in their upper-teens and early twenties. Heather suddenly regretted having demonized Brittany for knowing about Max's disappearance. She genuinely cared. Plus, she'd just lost her father. Heather had never known her father, not really and thusly, she couldn't fully comprehend the weight of that loss.

She had lost Max, though; she had seen echoes of this pain through her daughters' eyes. Perhaps all pain was somehow related. Perhaps you could link it all together in a spider web of horrible feelings. Heather couldn't say for sure. She had always longed to write adult fiction, but she'd ended up with children's fiction, storybooks, and that had suited her just fine. The extended metaphors were someone else's game.

"I hope to see you all after the service so that we can unite and talk about our favorite stories that involve this truly wonderful man," the preacher continued later. He then lifted his chin and closed his eyes as he said, "Thank you, oh Lord, for the gift of Joseph's life. We appreciated it for all it was and know he's in a better place now. Bar Harbor wouldn't be the same without him. And we'll keep our little town safe moving forward, just the way Joe would have wanted."

BACK IN THE CAR, Heather latched her seatbelt and gave her sister a sidelong glance. "Do you really believe everything the preacher said about Uncle Joe?" Immediately after she'd said it, regret shadowed her heart.

Nicole heaved a sigh and turned the key in the ignition. "I know you and Casey have this firm belief that the entire Keating family are monsters. But he wasn't. You could interview all of these people and hear countless stories about the goodness of Uncle Joe's heart." There was an edge to Nicole's voice, something that made Heather hesitant. "I mean, he welcomed me back in after years of just, you know, taking the money that was set aside for us after Dad passed. Month after month, we never questioned it and never thanked anyone for it."

"Thanked anyone? Were we supposed to thank someone after Dad abandoned us and then ended his own life—" Heather pointed out.

But Nicole waved a hand through the air to silence Heather. "When I arrived in Bar Harbor, after everything that had happened with Michael, with my kids grown and off at college, I just felt so alone in this world. Uncle Joe sat with me at one of the lowest points in my life. He took my hand, and he asked me how I was. It sounds so silly, yet so simple. But nobody had bothered asking me how I was for so long, and I—"

Nicole gasped for air. Heather's heart felt gripped with sorrow. She reached for Nicole's hand, but she resisted it. Again, Heather's cheeks burned with shame.

"I should have been there for you, even more, Nic," Heather whispered.

"You had your own stuff to deal with. I know that."

Their eyes dropped again toward their thighs. Outside, a baby screeched, and the sound of it joined the Northeastern howl of the wind as it whipped off Frenchman Bay.

There was so much to say. They couldn't possibly attack it all in one day.

They drove back to the inn and Eatery in silence. Heather dropped her head back on the car seat; her skull felt terribly heavy, as though her neck couldn't possibly lift again. They paused at a stoplight, where she watched as the wind whipped at the light itself, threatening to tug it off the line.

"Hard to believe it's the end of August," Heather stated, as though that meant anything at all.

Nicole made a soft sound in her throat, then pressed on the gas and shot them back across town. Heather turned to watch the little unique houses as they rushed past in many shades, their roofs pointed toward the grey sky above. In the driver's seat, Nicole began to weep again; the sounds were terribly soft, as though she tried her best to keep the cries hidden. Heather closed her eyes and lifted a hand to wrap over Nicole's.

So many years ago, when she, Nicole, and Casey had lived with their Aunt Tracy in Portland, they'd had a kind of system when one of them broke down. As children, they'd had a great deal to cry about. Their father had left them; soon after, he'd left the world; after that, their mother had died, as well. Their Aunt Tracy had been their entire world. And in the wake of that reality, they'd built up boundaries between their hearts and the rest of the world. This, she supposed, was where the promise never to make contact with Bar Harbor had come from.

And the fact that Nicole had come here and broken that pact? It still bothered her. But she was numb and oddly curious about it. She couldn't feel the rage that Casey felt. Casey had always been the hot-headed one. What one had Heather been all that time? She wasn't sure. Maybe the emotional one or the mentally unstable one. The one on the verge of some sort of depressive collapse.

THE FOLLOWING DAY, Heather stepped into the Acadia Eatery to find it in a state of chaos. Nicole hovered near the back in deep conversation with one of the servers. A table of thirteen howled with laughter in the corner while other diners clacked their forks against their platters of gorgeous-looking, high-end food. Although it was called an "Eatery," Heather had read that it was tongue-in-cheek; in actuality, this "Eatery" was fine dining at its best.

The Eatery was attached to the rest of the inn, but it had an even more elegant air to it, with beautiful windows that swept up across the ceiling and upper part of the far wall, which offered a dynamic view of the seemingly ever-changing, green mountains beyond. Nicole spotted Heather and finished up her conversation, then ducked down to meet her. Her smile was difficult to read.

"Finally made it for lunch," Nicole said. She'd been inviting Heather to dine since her arrival, but Heather had insisted on grabbing a sandwich to go, then hide out in her room. Something about her arrival to Bar Harbor had exhausted her. She supposed it had something to do with the fact that she hadn't done anything more than walk from her bed to the kitchen and back for the previous multiple months.

"I thought I'd give it a try," Heather offered, although that wasn't truly why she had come.

Nicole gestured toward a table for two in the far corner. "Maybe I could join you in a while?"

Heather flinched. The thought of sitting there at that table, of eating in public like this, of stuffing herself full under her sister's watchful eye, filled her with sorrow and fear. Nicole sensed her hesitation.

"What's wrong?" Nicole's nostrils flared.

"It's just, I mean, you had said something about Uncle Joe keeping some of— erm, Dad's things?"

Nicole arched an eyebrow. "You don't want to waste any time, do you?"

How could Heather describe it? That the existence of these boxes had burned a hole in her mind all this time? Plus, since Brittany had mentioned her father had liked to write, Heather had swam through strange emotions, painting suddenly a portrait of her father with far more similarities to her than she'd realized.

Depression. A writer's mentality. Maybe if she could peer into her father's soul through his words and things, she could find a way to heal herself.

Maybe not, though.

"I don't know if I have time for this," Nicole said pointedly. "So much going on today at the inn."

"I can sift through it on my own."

Silence bubbled between them. Nicole looked on the verge of saying something else, maybe that now, after spending a few days with Heather and her tenuous psyche, looking through their dad's things wasn't recommendable.

"I'll have someone show you the way. There's a lot of junk down there," Nicole finally offered. She turned her head quickly, as precisely as a robot, then lifted a finger toward a man who'd just charged into the Eatery, carrying several boxes of vegetables and fruits.

"Luke! Hey!"

The man stopped short. His grey eyes turned toward hers as he nodded. "What's up?"

"Could you show my sister the storage room downstairs?" Nicole asked. "There's a pile of boxes labeled with Adam's name on them. Maybe you've seen them down there."

CHAPTER FOUR

LUKE INTRODUCED himself properly after they were out of eye and ear shot of Nicole. His hand was welcoming and warm, the palm thick and his fingers so long that they dwarfed Heather's tiny hand as she shook his. They stood in the hall between the Eatery and the rest of the Keating Inn as a healthy August rain pattered across the rooftop.

"We can't seem to fight this rain," he said as a crooked smile dragged up toward his left ear.

"It's soothing," Heather heard herself say.

Luke's smile faltered the slightest bit. He dropped her hand as his grey eyes caught the slight light from the glittering rain. "You sure you're brave enough to go in the storage room? I try my best never to go down there. I'm not one for superstition, not really, but I don't like to tempt ghosts. And if there's anywhere you're tempting ghosts, it's down there."

"I can shield you if it comes to that," Heather told him.

Luke laughed outright. When was the last time she'd made a man laugh? Actually, when had she last made anyone laugh, least of all a man? Her smile shrunk, and he seemed to recognize the sinister pain behind all of this as he, too, calmed and turned himself toward the basement door.

"But it's New England," he interjected as he leafed through his pocket for the key. "I suppose having ghosts is a part of the equation."

He said it as though he wasn't from New England at all. Perhaps in another reality, Heather might have asked him about that, about where he was from. But her tongue felt glued to the top of her mouth; her anxiety shot through the roof.

The staircase was sinister and dark, with a single hanging exposed lightbulb. Luke yanked the string and cast a small beam of light across the steps before them. Heather grabbed her phone and used the Flashlight app to create a pool of light all the way down the stairs.

"Pshh. Technology," Luke teased. "What is it good for? We got along just fine with these rinky-dink lightbulbs. I mean, don't tell that to the multiple people who probably broke their legs on these stairs, but..." He laughed as he practically hopped and skipped down the rickety staircase while Heather took delicate steps behind. He was another of these overzealous creatures, people with such emotional fireworks happening within them that their excitement sizzled outward, affecting the world around them.

Heather had once felt akin to that sort of person. She'd had so many creative ideas, so much love, so much nerve that she'd poured it all into the books— and made a small fortune because of it. That person, the person she'd once been, now seemed like a foreigner. It wasn't the person who now walked delicately down the stairs.

"Here we are." Luke stood before the large pile of boxes and tapped a broad hand across the scrawled word ADAM. "Adam's your dad, I guess?"

"Yes, he is," Heather answered, not making eye contact with him. A moment later, she locked eyes, giving him a soft smile. "But I hardly know a thing about the guy."

"Hmm. That sucks," Luke affirmed. Somehow, that was all he had to say. He then passed her the key and said, "I'm sorry to do this to you, but Nicole will serve my head for dinner if I'm not back in the kitchen. Sous chef, you know."

"Ah. The ultimate kitchen slave," Heather replied as she tapped the key against the side of her nose.

"Something like that. You'll be okay down here?"

"Just me and the ghosts to keep me company," she quipped. "What more could I want?"

Uncle Joe had set aside three boxes of Adam's things. Three boxes were the last remaining items of the man's long life, the last echoing of his long-lost soul. When the last of Luke's footfalls disappeared, Heather pulled the first box off the top. With it came a rush of dust. She coughed as she placed the box down, then smeared her hand over her nose. Since the books had started to make actual money, she'd hardly spent much time with dust, as she'd hired a housekeeper to keep her space spick and span. Dust, therefore, reminded her of those long-ago shoestring-budget years. It made her ache with sorrow. Funnily enough, it made her miss Max.

But everything did.

The first box was filled to the top with books. *Death in Venice* by Thomas Mann, Beckett plays, Shakespeare, Melville's *Moby Dick*— the list of classics went on. It seemed such a tragedy to Heather that books of such caliber were kept underground. Why were they in Adam's box? Perhaps they had been his favorites; perhaps his brother couldn't have parted with them, as they represented Adam's inner life.

She moved on to the next box. It was smaller, filled with old papers, many of which were signed by Adam himself. She had never seen his signature, and the sight of it both thrilled her and shocked her. It was such an everyday thing, signing your name. How remarkable that one day, you wouldn't be around to sign it; your signature would exist only in memory, on silly, useless forms.

Alongside these papers, she found three old diaries, all bound with dark brown leather and extremely worn. Her heart skipped a beat. She flipped to the first page, where she found an old, yellowed newspaper clipping, which Uncle Joe had obviously snipped out.

The headline read:

Exhausted Restaurateur Adam Keating Commits Suicide

Heather's heart rate picked up as her eyes scanned the headline a second time. In the clipping, Adam's face peered back at her— a photo taken long before his death, when his eyes had gleamed, little pockets of hope.

"Hi, Dad," she whispered. Her throat caught. "I'm here, now. I'm really here."

She wasn't sure why she spoke to him like that. She supposed, in her current emotional state, she might have cried at anything. All the people they'd lost along the way. Max, her mother, her Aunt Tracy and the original loss: Adam Keating, her father.

One of the diaries was thinner. When she opened it, she realized that it wasn't a diary at all. It seemed her father had been experimenting with short stories across many different genres. The first was a fantasy story about ogres, giants, fairies, and dragons; another spoke about outer space, about a trip to the moon that would ultimately save his family here on earth. There were poems and little jokes, along with incomplete paragraphs that seemed to capture only the wild, chaotic urgings of his mind and nothing else. As she read, Heather recognized a bit of her own soul in his sense of humor and his style of writing.

It was just as Brittany had said. He'd always been writing, and here was a real record of his talent.

Why hadn't he pursued it the way she had? She supposed he'd been bound by circumstance, caught in whatever web of life he'd found himself in. There was no way to truly know why he had taken his own life. He was a stranger, and here she was, as a sort of archaeologist, trying to stitch together the pieces she could find of this man and discover something more. It wasn't clear what this would do for her, if it would fulfill her in any way at all. She just knew she had to.

Still, it was so nourishing to read these little stories, to feel the way his mind might have worked.

Suddenly exhausted, Heather collapsed on the ground, gathered her legs in a cross, and moved on to the next leather-bound book. This, she found, was a diary, dated throughout a few years prior to Heather's own birth. Casey was the only baby at the time; Adam and their mother, Jane, were young parents. But there was none of the bright energy Heather remembered from her early days of parenting the girls. Alongside her exhaustion, she'd swam with light and color and excitement as Bella and Kristine had taught her heart to grow beyond any size she'd ever envisioned.

An entry from a dark, wretched patch in early January of a long-ago year read:

Casey kept us awake all night. I took her in my arms when Jane started to cry as well— and I gazed down at this perfect little baby, this innocent form, and felt nothing but terror. This creature is in my care, yet I feel completely ill-equipped, sometimes, even to care for myself. Here we are in the early days. This baby knows only eat - sleep - cry. But what next? When she can walk or when she can run — when all the terrors of the world turn their face to her, hungry for whatever she can give them?

Why did I ever imagine myself to be strong enough to be a father? I should have never put myself in this position. And I think Jane sees my weakness, too. Women always see it in you; they can smell it, too. I can't even pretend to be this strong, masculine creature around her. I can hardly put the baby to sleep; how can I possibly provide?

Heather shivered at his ramblings. It was clear he was something of an intellectual, a poet, a man troubled with sinister aching and unsettling ideas. Obviously, he'd stuck around with Casey, as he and their mother had gone on to have Nicole and then Heather. Probably, his inner demons had only grown darker with each new daughter.

Her eyes filled with tears yet again, but she held them back. "What happened to you?" she whispered to herself as she continued through his ramblings, through the horrors of being the late man, Adam Keating.

She flipped toward the back of the diary and soon realized that this was just a single year in Adam's life. The other diary, however, was empty, as was another leather-bound book within the box. Why, given his love for writing, had Adam only kept a diary of one year of his life? It didn't make sense.

When she lifted the last empty leather-bound book, a folded-up piece of paper fluttered out of the front cover. It landed smack-dab in the center of the grey basement floor, and Heather had to strain herself to reach out for it and grip the edge. When she lifted it, she found a beautiful handwriting, different than Adam's, although no less romantic.

Just a single line was scribed at the top of the folded-up piece of paper.

Let's meet, Adam. Bring the baby. J.

Heather's heart fluttered. J? Did this mean Jane, Adam's wife and Heather's mother? Slowly, she turned the paper over to find that the other side of the letter was filled with Adam's handwriting, although this handwriting was far more frantic and scattered than the handwriting in the journal.

The letter was written to Jane, Heather's mother.

Jane,

There's no reason you should read this letter. I'm rather sure you hate me, and why wouldn't you? I wronged you in ways I pledged not to wrong you; I belittled your suffering in the face of my own selfishness and lust; and now, on this dark and stormy night in Bar Harbor, I find myself aching for you, all the way in Portland, in ways that I never imagined I would.

You were the only woman I could ever trust, Jane. That fact alone makes me feel like a very small, very weak-minded man. But you always knew I was small and weak-minded, didn't you? Perhaps I resented you for that.

I find myself in a very difficult situation. I can already feel you rolling your eyes at this concept— that naturally, Adam Keating is in a difficult situation, as I always am and always will be. I know; I do it to myself. But now, it's not only me at play here.

It's just me and this baby, here—a toddler. And I find myself suffering in much the same way as I did with Casey when she was a baby, but I don't have the support I had with you. I'm all alone, and I fear what will befall this baby if I don't find some resolve.

I beg of you, Jane. Will you meet me? I want to discuss the potential that you help me with this poor, innocent child— this child who asked for none of this yet is left with the horror of my lackluster abilities. As you know, I can love with my whole heart and mind, but when it comes to actual physical care, I'm a bit at a loss.

She's beautiful, Jane. Maybe it pains you to read that, but it's true. She's got jet-black hair and these bright blue eyes. She's happy and healthy, with a little round mole, right under her chin. When she looks at me, she always laughs as though we're sharing a joke. I feel like an imbecile. I feel so lost.

Write me back, Jane. You don't have to forgive me, not ever, if only you'll help me and, mostly, my dilemma.

Eternally yours,

Adam

Heather allowed the paper to flutter back to the ground. She gaped at it as though it was a bomb on the verge of explosion. "No. No— no." Heather wrapped her hand around her throat as it tightened and threatened to choke her. If she screamed all the way down there in the basement, nobody would hear her.

Did this mean...

Could it possibly mean...

That her mother was not, in fact, her mother?

Then who was?

CHAPTER FIVE

THE FOLLOWING hour or so left Heather feeling in a kind of daydream. She collected the diaries, the letter, the newspaper clipping, and the book that contained her father's stories in one of the boxes, slipped it under her arm, and then made her way up the steps to the ground floor. There, she latched the door tightly behind her with a key as her knees knocked together. Three maids hustled past, gossiping about one of the other maids and her seeming lack of ability to put the beds together correctly. "It's lazy, is what it is," one of them announced. Not one of them eyed her; none seemed to notice that Heather's cheeks had lost their color or that her world had suddenly spun off its axis and into the great beyond. If she was the child Adam Keating was talking about in that letter, then that meant her life was no longer the way she had always envisioned it prior to this moment.

When Heather had decided to come to Bar Harbor to witness her father's world, to understand more of him and his decisions, she hadn't envisioned that her entire order of the universe would disintegrate. She had assumed she'd read a few lines of a diary, hear a few stories, then feel this oneness with her deceased father in a way that would allow her to patch up her broken heart and continue on her journey. She had even envisioned herself writing a book about the experience set in Bar Harbor. Now she felt even more confused and maybe a little frightened at what she might find.

Heather collapsed at a two-person table in the Eatery. She positioned the box of diaries along her feet. Luke rushed past in his chef whites and winked at her as he asked, "Find anything juicy down there?"

Heather struggled to draw up a smile. Before she could, Luke continued into the ever-whipping kitchen door and disappeared. Nicole's voice rang out a moment later. Heather glanced up as Nicole headed out into the empty dining room, removing her apron as she went.

"There she is," Nicole said brightly. "I kept expecting you to come up to grab something to eat. You missed the lunch rush completely."

Heather grimaced. How long had she been in the basement? Had she lost her grip on time?

"Anyway." Nicole hovered at Heather's table as her smile faltered. "I'll put together a plate for you."

"That sounds good." They studied one another. Nicole's face now seemed entirely foreign to Heather. She had known Nicole's face for her entire life, she'd thought. She had known the little ways that it twitched when Nicole grew nervous or grew broad and vibrant when she laughed.

But was Nicole only Heather's half-sister, after all this time?

Had she not even known Nicole until she was a toddler? She lifted a finger to the mole just beneath her chin, the one her father had described in the letter, and shuddered.

"You okay, hon?" Nicole asked, her brows knitted with concern.

Heather made a small noise in her throat.

"Did you find something in Dad's stuff?" Nicole asked again.

"A few things. I don't know. I'm going to bring it home and go over it more," Heather finally said.

"Great."

"Great," Heather echoed. She could feel the lie simmering beneath the surface.

"Okay, well." Nicole's eyes flashed back toward the kitchen. "I'll go make you a plate, and maybe we can catch up tonight? It feels like since you got here, we've been missing each other."

In truth, Heather had had to sleep far more than normal; she had skipped out on dinners together; she'd avoided Nicole as best as she could for fear that Nicole would demand her to stop with her depressive episode. She wasn't the sort of person to tell Heather to just "get over" Max's death; still, Heather was hyper-conscious of how annoying she was in her current state.

Nicole left her table and again disappeared into the kitchen. Heather returned her gaze to her thighs. Anxiety spiraled through her body. She suddenly reached for her father's box of things, then shot toward the hallway between the Eatery and the inn. There, she pressed the box against the glass and forced herself to take deep breaths.

"Come on, pull yourself together," she rasped.

There were footfalls behind her— maids and caterers and other staff members as they rushed back and forth. Many of them were in conversation, saying humdrum things that made Heather increasingly jealous. She suddenly wished she could care about something like the linens in room 233; she wished she could dive into the daily tasks in the Eatery kitchen, chop carrots and onions into infinity. She wished she wasn't, currently, herself.

"How is this possible?" she whispered again to herself. "How— after all this time, can my mother not be my mother?"

"...What did you just say?"

The words came out of the darkness, right behind her. Heather froze with fear. Slowly, she twitched around to find Luke behind her, still, all dressed in his chef whites, holding what looked to be the plate Nicole had made for her for lunch. His eyes glowed with curiosity as he lifted the plate.

Heather dropped the box of diaries. It made a thud sound when it hit the ground, then fell to the side to spill the books across the floor. Luke hurriedly positioned the plate on one hand and fell to one knee to put the books back in the box. Heather remained frozen as she gaped at him.

"You heard me."

Luke righted the box and then placed the platter of what looked to be vegetarian lasagna in her outstretched hands. His eyes found hers.

"I guess I shouldn't have."

Heather's heart pounded away in her chest. Suddenly, the weight of her secret had found its way onto this man's shoulders. She felt lighter as a result, which was something she hadn't expected. Hurriedly, she gripped his wrist and led him toward the far end of the hallway so that her eyes remained on the Eatery, where Nicole was in conversation with another worker.

"I just found a letter from my father to the woman I thought was my mother. It makes me think that maybe, maybe, my mother raised me before she died, but she was never actually my blood relation," she explained.

Luke nodded contemplatively. "And why wouldn't you want Nicole to know that?"

How could she possibly answer this? How could she possibly explain that she hoped, with everything she was, that the letter was somehow false? Jane was her mother; Jane had always been her mother. It was just as Casey had said— it had always been Casey, Nicole, and Heather against the world. What if Heather was the odd sister out? What if she was only part of them and the other part was foreign?

"I don't know," Heather admitted finally. "I just want to make sure it's real before I say anything."

He squared his shoulders. "How will you do that?"

Heather kneeled on the ground to hunt again for the letter. Why did she want to trust this man? But suddenly, he felt like her only light in the darkness. With a quivering hand, she showed Luke the letter that explained that Adam was in Bar Harbor with a toddler that very much seemed like her. "But I've always been told that I was born in Portland," she explained. "While Casey and Nicole were born here, before the four of them moved."

"Huh." Luke placed his hands on his hips and turned his gorgeous grey eyes toward the window. Outside, thunder clapped wildly and made the glass shake. "I have a friend who works in the records department here in Bar Harbor."

"Do you?" Heather's heart pattered wildly.

"If your birth certificate is here in Bar Harbor, I could find out about it," he continued.

Heather's throat tightened. She didn't like the idea of Luke roaming through the records without her. She wanted to be sure. "Take me with you."

LATER THAT EVENING, Heather changed into a pair of flannel pants and a t-shirt and sauntered into the little living room of the beautiful house on the edge of the grounds, where she found Nicole bent over a book. She had dotted a pair of glasses at the bottom of her nose, and her lips moved slightly as she read. Heather hesitated before she spoke. Memories flashed through her. Throughout their youth together, Heather had been a year behind Nicole in school. Nicole had always been just a tiny bit ahead— in math, in reading, in music, only because of this slight age gap. Now, Heather was reminded of being maybe five or six and watching Nicole get better and better at reading while she still floundered. Their mother, Jane, had taken Heather on her lap and said, "You'll get there before you know it. And the best part of it is that Nicole will help you learn! That's the thing about sisters. They're always there for you when you need help."

She supposed that had been especially true for Jane when Jane herself had passed away— and Aunt Tracy had picked up the slack as their stand-in mother. Their life with Aunt Tracy had been vibrant and beautiful; they'd loved her almost like a mother. Still, Casey, Nicole, and Heather had all ached with the memory of the woman they had lost. Jane. Who on earth was this woman? This woman who'd lied? And had Aunt Tracy known about this, too?

"What are you doing?" Nicole had noticed Heather's presence. She placed a bookmark in her book and sat up, adjusting her glasses across the bridge of her nose. Her smile was inquisitive.

"Oh, just thinking." Heather fell back in a green chair and placed a slender leg over the other.

"About what?"

How could she possibly name it?

"About Uncle Joe," Heather lied. "I can't believe you got to know him over the past few months."

Nicole folded her hands over her lap. "Honestly, it was one of the biggest blessings I could have given myself."

Heather pressed her lips together tightly. "I know you said Uncle Joe didn't talk about Dad much, since it was so painful. But do you remember anything?"

She had a suspicion that Nicole already knew about what she'd discovered and that she had decided to keep it a secret as well. Was there a way Heather could signal her that she knew already?

"Oh, gosh. He told me some really funny stories from their youth," Nicole remarked. "They were rascals, always getting into trouble. And apparently, they both had motorcycles and rocketed all over the great state of Maine before the age of eighteen. Our grandmother called them adventurers."

"Wow," Heather breathed. "Sounds like something in the movies."

Silence fell between them. Nicole rubbed her teeth against her lower lip. "I'm sorry I didn't tell you to come sooner. Before Uncle

Joe passed, I should have brought you here. I knew you were—well..."

"Struggling?"

Nicole shrugged. "But I knew you and Casey were resistant. And I felt so guilty for breaking our promise."

Heather waved a hand. "Let's not talk about that anymore."

Again, silence. Nicole lifted the remote control and suggested they watch a movie together. As they flicked through a streaming service, they talked about Casey and her recent, passive-aggressive messages.

"Do you think she'll ever forgive us for coming here?" Nicole asked.

Heather laughed. "You know Casey. She can forgive, but she can never forget."

"It's true. She's got a record of our wrongs about a mile long," Nicole glanced at her with a grin. "But I guess that's the way sisters work. Mom always talked about that. About how important your sisters are. What was it she said? That they'll love you more than you'll ever love yourself, but they'll also point out every single way you're wrong for the rest of your days."

Heather felt the heaviness of the words. Nicole and Casey were her sisters; she'd known no other life. And this "Mom" person? What she'd potentially learned today made her memories feel horrific. How could she trust herself or the visions she still had of her mother?

CHAPTER SIX

IT HAD BEEN A SLEEPLESS NIGHT. Heather was accustomed to these. Those dark nights after Max's disappearance into the depths of the ocean had cast her into a similar spell. She'd spent hours tossing herself beneath the sheets as sweat pooled across her stomach and between her breasts. Always, she'd walked to the bathroom mirror to toss water on her cheeks and blink at her reflection. A sad, lonely woman who couldn't even figure out the basic how-tos on keeping herself alive and healthy. That's who peered back.

It was September 1st, and Bar Harbor had drawn a glorious morning for them— complete with egg-shell blue skies and glowing sunlight that crept through the still-green leaves in the fluttering trees. Heather sat on the back porch of the little green house with a mug of steaming coffee. It was just past seven, and she could hear Nicole fidgeting around in the kitchen. There was the jangle of her keys, a rough step as she turned back toward the toaster to remove her nearly-burnt toast. In a moment, Nicole appeared in the view of the glass door, a piece of toast between her teeth and her smile seen on either side, just behind.

"Hey there," Heather greeted as Nicole stepped through the glass door. "You're a sight for sore eyes."

Nicole chuckled as she performed a little juggle, placing her mug of coffee on the table, taking a full bite of toast, then pressing herself into the chair alongside Heather. When she swallowed, she asked, "And what are you up to today? I feel awful that I haven't taken you around to see any of the sights. We should plan a beach day before it gets too cold or go into the mountains for a hike."

The thought of these nearly-strenuous activities made Heather's heart drop.

"Yeah. Maybe," she said. "Today, though, I thought I'd just head into Bar Harbor. Maybe check out a book shop or two and write in a coffee shop— that kind of thing."

Why did she feel it so necessary to lie? Oh, but the light that curved out of Nicole's eyes at this moment pleased her.

"That's incredible, Heather. Seriously. You always used to tell me that you got such inspiration from going into bookshops," she beamed. "I teased you that time, saying you stole your ideas there, and you burst into tears."

Heather rolled her eyes. "I was maybe fifteen? Right? Super hormonal and very self-conscious about anything my older sister said to me?"

Nicole giggled. "I guess Casey and I were never as emotional as you. But it's why you're in the arts to this day." She paused and then grabbed a little pad of paper off to the left, where she began to scribe a list. "Here are a few really cool spots in town. I think you'll die for this coffee shop. They have these brilliant little oat cookies. They remind me of the ones Aunt Tracy used to make." She paused as the memory fell over both of them like a blanket. "I've tried to imitate them, but they never come out just right. Too crunchy."

Their Aunt Tracy had passed away only a couple of years before. She had been their last link to family, on their mother's side. Heather had a hunch that Aunt Tracy's death had pushed Nicole to reach out to their Uncle Joe, although she couldn't be sure.

"Well, anyway. I have to hit the road," Nicole finally said as the silence continued on between them. Her eyebrows twitched with confusion.

Just as they'd agreed, Luke picked Heather up at the far end of the long driveway that snaked from the main road, all the way to the Keating House. Heather waited as the truck wheels crept to a halt before she whipped a hand up to the door handle and eased herself into the much-higher front seat. She wasn't accustomed to massive trucks like this.

"Not bad for a girl from Portland," Luke teased as she finally adjusted herself.

Heather laughed. "Maybe from Portland. Maybe not. I guess today will tell the tale."

Luke drove them back east, then north into the town of Bar Harbor. The radio station in his truck spit, then fizzed, until he adjusted it back to an oldies' station. His whistle was vibrant as they drove into Bar Harbor. He spread his hand out toward the view of the gorgeous water, which glowed from the bright light of the confident blue sky above.

"I never get sick of this view," he confessed. "No matter how long I'm here. I'm still a Midwestern boy to my core and amazed by everything else."

"Midwestern?" Heather arched an eyebrow with surprise. "What brought you all the way up here?"

Luke laughed as though he had about a zillion little secrets up his sleeve and planned not to share a single one with her. This intrigued Heather, in a way. It had been a long time since she'd felt any sort of curiosity— yet here and now, with her father's diaries and this letter and this Midwestern man, her mind found new reasons to latch.

"I guess there's a lot to say there. And also not so much," Luke affirmed. He drove the truck down a side road, then slid up to an official-looking government building. He turned off the engine and turned his grey eyes toward her. "You ready to figure this out?"

She flashed him an uncertain grin. "Ready as I'll ever be."

They jumped out of the truck. Heather was surprised at the warm tinge of the air. Somehow, her brain had already made peace with the fact that autumn approached. The fast-approaching darkness and depression were nothing new to her. But right now, the sunlight demanded something else.

They entered the building. Luke lifted a hand in greeting to the person who seemed to be his "friend," a young woman in her early thirties, it seemed like, with overly-blonde hair and blue eyes that shone like little pools. Heather felt a funny stab of jealousy. She guessed it was just the presence of such a young, vibrant woman, with her entire life ahead of her. She'd never lost her husband in such a substantial accident on the ocean. Her life was cotton candy and rainbows, probably.

"Hi, Monica," Luke greeted as he rapped his hands across the counter.

"Hey there, stranger." Monica's teeth were overly large, too. Was that attractive? "It's been a while since I saw you at the bar."

Luke's smile was mischievous. "I've had a whole lot of work up at the Eatery. Working as a sous chef now."

Monica's eyes gleamed. You could clearly see she was impressed. "Well, we miss you around there. Although I have to say, some people are pleased you're not around to beat them at darts."

Luke chuckled. Heather's impatience mounted.

Did they want to get a room?

"Anyway, I was curious if you could help me with those records." Luke smoothly slipped into this mode; it almost sounded flirtatious, as though it was linked to all the other conversations they'd had.

Ah! He was manipulating her for Heather's benefit. Her cheeks burned with a mix of gratefulness and fear.

"Oh, of course. It's a slow day around here," Monica affirmed. "I can show you the way."

Heather and Luke followed the sound of Monica's clacking heels all the way down the hallway, then off to the right. They entered a room that had many shelves, all filled with boxes that were labeled with birth records, death records, wills, deeds, information about the mountains and the national parks, and everything in between. Luke whistled again and said, "It's pretty impressive that you're in charge of all this, Monica."

Monica whipped her hair behind her shoulder. "It's a big responsibility."

Heather was reminded of a child, always looking for attention in this way. She had to force herself not to roll her eyes.

"I'll just be up at the front desk," she affirmed. "Let me know if you need anything."

"Sure thing, Mon," Luke said with a wink. "Thanks a bunch."

When Monica disappeared, Heather lifted her eyes toward Luke's and made a funny face.

"What?" Luke asked, his eyes twinkling. He knew exactly what her face was about.

"Nothing." She wanted to tell him that he would have made a good investigator— that he could easily slip in and out of situations and manipulate people. But in truth, she didn't know him at all, and even more than that, she wasn't sure her words would come out as flirtatious, the way she wanted them to be. She couldn't trust herself.

In the silence that followed, Luke shrugged and then asked, "So. What month and date and year are we looking for?"

Heather headed toward the birth certificate section, where she dropped down to 1977— the year she'd been born. "My birthday is in February," she told him. Her finger ticked along the multiple boxes until she found the month. She then dragged the box out and leafed through the multiple documents, which were listed in alphabetical order. "I guess if I was actually born in Bar Harbor, I would have my father's last name— Keating."

"As opposed to?"

"I was Harvey as a kid," Heather explained. "We didn't want anything to do with my dad. Not until recently."

Luke nodded firmly as Heather continued to hunt. But soon, her hunt fell flat. February 1977 featured a number of other babies

— all of whom had lived on the planet just as long as Heather had, a full forty-four years. Her birth certificate was nowhere to be found.

"No record," she whispered. Her heartbeat sped up. "Maybe that means his letter is just ramblings? Maybe I was really born in Portland after all?"

She glanced up to find Luke's eyes. He gave a half-shrug.

"I know. It doesn't matter to you," she lamented as she placed the box back on the shelf.

"It does," Luke affirmed. "I know how horrible it feels to not belong to anything or anyone."

She turned and locked eyes with him. His swirled with emotion, and his words felt deep as if he had been wounded. Heather wanted to ask, to know more about his past now that he was being slightly vulnerable with her, but decided not to say anything instead. At that moment, there was the clicking of Monica's heels and then the bright flash of her hair in the doorway.

"Hey, Luke-y? Can you wrap up in here? My boss is about to come back, and he doesn't love it when people rifle around in the files."

LATER THAT NIGHT, Heather collapsed back in the house and flicked through channels on TV, waiting for Nicole's arrival back from the inn. In the wake of their unfortunate search that morning, she and Luke had wandered around Bar Harbor, both at a loss, hardly speaking. Heather had told him briefly about her work as a fantasy writer for young children and teens, which had fascinated him.

"For a long time, I didn't know you were allowed to do stuff in life that you actually wanted to do," he'd explained after that.

These words had thrilled and fascinated Heather. She'd never known herself to settle. Now that Luke worked as a sous chef, it seemed he had found his way to what he actually wanted. But what lurked in his past that made his eyes so somber sometimes?

Still, Heather felt she couldn't pry.

When Nicole entered, she was in a flurry of activity. She walked around the living room, dropped her purse on the opposite chair, and told a series of harrowing stories about the guests at the Keating Inn who'd tried their hand at destroying an entire suite. "I swear, I should know better by now than to let bachelor parties stay at the inn," Nicole groaned as she yanked her hair from its ponytail. "But they seemed so nice and sweet yesterday. You know, before the buckets of booze."

Heather couldn't be fully present in the conversation, not with the pressing weight of her fears. Slowly, Nicole recognized these worries lurking behind her eyes. They were sisters— or something like it. They could read one another like a book.

"What's wrong, Heather?" She dropped down on the chair across from her as Heather's face crumpled.

"I want to tell you. But I think we have to call Casey, too."

Nicole's hands shook as she gripped her tablet and dialed Casey. Heather could feel the fears race behind Nicole's eyes. Probably, she assumed Heather was about to announce a real illness — cancer or heart disease or something equally sinister.

Casey's face sprung up on the tablet. She looked disgruntled.

"There they are," she exasperated. "The women who turned their backs against me."

Heather's lower lip quivered. Immediately, Casey's face shifted to one of shock.

"Heather? Are you okay? What's going on?"

Nicole's shoulders dropped. She swung an arm around Heather, the youngest sister, and announced, "Heather apparently has something to tell us."

"Oh my God," Casey whispered.

Heather's heart banged in her chest. "It's not what you think," she tried. "But it's a huge shock to me. I did some digging in the basement of the Keating Inn, and I found an old letter. Dad wrote it to Mom, and it was addressed from Bar Harbor to Portland. The only reason it's here is because Mom just used the letter to write her response on the back. The letter is kind of a ramble— a real mess."

"Dad wasn't in his right mind, Heather," Casey whispered.

"I know that," Heather tried.

"He took his own life," Casey countered.

"I know. But this letter—" Heather lifted the letter itself from the binding of the leather book beside her. Nicole took it and began to read it furiously as Heather continued. "It basically insinuates that Dad was here in Bar Harbor with a toddler that had jet-black hair and a mole beneath her chin. And he asks Mom if she'll meet him and pleads to take the toddler."

Nicole's nostrils flared as she continued to read. Her eyes were like glass. Casey remained silent. When Nicole finished her read-through, she flipped the letter over and read Jane's words. A strange and low sound escaped her lips.

"What?" Casey demanded.

"Umm. It's weird. It's really weird." Nicole hung her head as she flipped the letter back over and re-read it.

"Come on. We can't just take this letter as proof of anything," Casey huffed with impatience.

Heather pressed her lips together as Casey continued to rattle out facts they knew about their father— that he was unreliable. That their mother and aunt hadn't ever had much good to say about him.

"Mom was just always so vocal about the three of us. Us three girls," Heather said finally. "I just can't get my mind around the idea that it might not be true. That it might be a lie."

Silence fell again. Nicole dropped her shoulders and lifted her chin toward the tablet to look at Casey again.

"Mom always said I was born in Portland," Heather said finally. "But today, I looked through the birth records here in Bar Harbor."

"Anything?" Casey asked.

"No," Heather admitted.

"Maybe I can do some investigating here," Casey offered. "Maybe we can even find proof that what Mom always said is true."

Heather's heart lifted. "That would be incredible, Case. Seriously."

"Anything for my baby sister," Casey said.

"That's what I'm terrified of," Heather breathed. "I'm terrified we're only half-sisters. I'm terrified that we're not—"

"Shh," Casey said. She waved a hand back and forth in front of the screen. "We don't know anything for sure yet." She then gave Heather a funny smile and said, "I told you not to go back to Bar Harbor, didn't I? Now, look what you've done. You've opened up a can of worms."

CHAPTER SEVEN

"UNCLE JOE KEPT the good wine in the cellar." Nicole appeared alongside Heather with a bottle of Primitivo lifted in one hand and two shining wine glasses in her other. Heather had spent the previous five minutes in a strained state, her eyes enormous and glued to the black television.

Heather shook her head in an attempt to clear the cobwebs. "Sorry. I think I was a million miles away."

"Come on. I put the space heater on the back porch." Nicole turned and headed out for the wrap-around porch, where she perched at the little wooden table, placed the wine bottle and glasses in front of her, then removed the cork with the flourish of the opener. "You look like you've spent all day with ghosts," Nicole pointed out as Heather joined her, wrapping herself up in flannel.

"I feel that I'm the ghost, actually," Heather told her.

Nicole tapped a hand across Heather's lower arm. "I don't know. You seem pretty solid to me."

Heather and Nicole clinked glasses and made eye contact. After their first sip, Heather turned her gaze out toward the Frenchman Bay just beyond, which was the color of ink. Far out, boats flashed their lights as they made their way across the vast ocean. Since Max's death, she hadn't been on the water, not once. Fear of the immense darkness beyond took hold of her, and she very nearly asked Nicole if they could return inside.

"So, you've kept all this to yourself the past few days?" Nicole finally pierced through Heather's cloudy thoughts.

"I didn't know how to tell you yet." How could Heather explain that she'd felt like such a foreigner since Max's death; now, she had to reckon with the fact that the way she'd envisioned her entire life might not have been correct.

"You don't have to hide stuff from me," Nicole told her softly.

"You're the one who kept that you'd come to Bar Harbor for so long," she pointed out.

Nicole's eyes dropped. "I knew you'd be angry with me. And you were."

"Maybe we should try to be honest from now on. As much as we can," Heather tried. Her eyes filled with tears as she added, "I just can't believe that all these years, I thought we were real sisters..."

Nicole splayed a hand over Heather's. Far in the distance, a boat blared its horn.

"You are my sister, Heather. Nothing will ever change that."

Heather swallowed the lump in her throat. "I keep coming back to the letter. I guess it means Dad had left Mom? And came back here to have some kind of affair? Is that rational?"

Nicole's eyes dropped. "Poor Mom. It must have destroyed her."

"But if she really raised me as her own— I mean, what a saint she was," Heather breathed. "And I never knew."

"How did you look through the birth records of Bar Harbor, anyway?" Nicole asked finally. "Seems like a pretty cagey thing to do."

"Oh." Heather's cheeks burned with sudden embarrassment. "Luke said he knew someone at the records office."

Nicole arched her eyebrow. "Luke? Eatery sous chef, Luke?"

"That's right."

"Huh." Nicole puffed out her cheeks, then added, "Okay. Just. Well..."

"What?"

"Just be careful, I guess."

"Of Luke?"

"He's a great guy, one of the best and an excellent worker. He just has a tricky past. I'm not totally sure he can overcome it," Nicole returned.

Heather arched an eyebrow with curiosity, yet again held back her questions. It didn't seem her place to dig. Besides, she had her own personal digging to do within her own messed-up life.

"The girl at the city records place looked at him like he was the sun and the moon put together," Heather admitted with a funny smile.

"Luke is beloved around here," Nicole affirmed. "And I guess I don't blame all those girls. He's a handsome guy, very friendly and reliable, to a point."

"But you've never thought of him like that?" Heather wasn't sure why she asked.

Nicole shook her head almost violently. "He was around during those first few months as I got to know Uncle Joe. You could tell that Uncle Joe looked at Luke like a son; since he treated me almost like a long-lost daughter, it just never occurred to me to see him like that."

Heather took a long sip of wine and allowed the dark, dry wine to coat the back of her tongue. "I regret that I missed out on Uncle Joe, especially now. He could have told me so much, explained so much. I never imagined that our own stories would be lost when other people died. But I guess that happens naturally."

Nicole nodded. "Do you think Dad was actually crazy when he wrote that letter?"

"It's difficult to say," Heather returned. "But he didn't take his life for another few years after that. I guess that makes me think, maybe, he was still in a decent frame of mind. But who's to say? This was all so, so long ago."

CASEY CALLED THE FOLLOWING AFTERNOON. Heather was perched on a bench that overlooked Frenchman Bay with a book propped up on her thigh. Wind flourished through her jet-black curls as she lifted her phone and tried to make peace, already, with whatever news Casey had.

"Hey there."

Casey's voice was high-pitched. "Hey, I managed to speak to someone with access to the records of Maine Medical."

Heather didn't bother asking how Casey had done it; Casey Harvey was Casey Harvey. She'd always gotten her way.

"That was the hospital that Mom said you were born at, right?" Casey asked.

"Yes, it is."

"Well, they have no record of anyone by the name of Heather Harvey," Casey returned. "Nor of a Heather Keating—there's nothing."

Heather's heart sank to the bottom of her chest. "Huh."

"I'm sorry. I wish I had better news," Casey told her.

"Me too."

They held the silence. Another wind rushed against the receiver and blew sound all the way to Portland.

"It sounds cold there," Casey told her.

"Chilly, I guess."

Casey heaved a sigh. "Do you regret going to Bar Harbor now?"

"I don't know," Heather answered truthfully. "Maybe a little bit. If I say I regret that, though, then I'd have to say I regret almost everything else. I feel a bit like a lost cause, making these aimless decisions, ending up in different situations, but not really feeling them. You know?"

Again, Casey was quiet. Heather knew she'd worried her. But how else was she meant to speak about the horror of Max's death? How else could she deal with it without describing it?

"So I guess this means Mom was lying," Casey stated finally.

"I guess so."

"I never took her to be a liar," Casey admitted, her words laced with frustration.

"It's like you took the words right out of my mouth," Heather returned. She stitched her teeth again over her lower lip. "As a mother, I know I lied here and there over the years, but only to protect the girls."

"I thought about that, too. How there must have been a good reason."

They exchanged a few more words, most of which meant nothing at all. Heather's mind was elsewhere; Casey seemed to feel guilty about all of it, although it wasn't her fault in the slightest. Finally, Casey said she had to run. Heather pressed the phone against her chest as a crisp autumn wind rushed across her cheeks.

Heather zipped her sweatshirt up to her chin. Her mind returned yet again to Adam's diary. It had been extensive, something he had updated regularly throughout that year. It stood to reason that there were other diaries, but where? Perhaps they'd been tossed in a landfill somewhere. Perhaps the answers to her questions had rotted out long ago.

At the top of the hill that overlooked Bar Harbor, she turned and blinked out across the cottages, which dotted the land en route toward the vibrant glow of the sea. Why had she and Max come here, all those years ago, before their babies? She remembered telling him that there was darkness in Bar Harbor for her— a part of herself she would never look at too deeply for fear of what it would reveal. Max had told her there wasn't a past any longer; there was only whatever future they could create together. But her future with Max had been ripped away from her. Now, her past, too, was disintegrating. What was she left with?

Heather walked up the steps and back into the Keating Inn. Jackie stood at the front desk with a pencil between her teeth as she typed something into the computer. Jackie's eyes flipped up to catch Heather; her smile made her pencil fall.

"There she is!" Jackie beamed in greeting. "How are you finding our little slice of heaven so far?"

Heather realized to onlookers that she seemed nothing but a tourist on a family vacation. She found a smile and replied, "It's really one of the more remarkable places I've ever been." Maybe that was true, in a sense. After all, she felt much different than she had prior to her arrival.

"So good to hear," Jackie affirmed. "I've known your Uncle Joe for years and years, you know? And I have memories of your father running around Bar Harbor years back. He was a good deal older than me. Guess he never gave me the time of day. But he was widely known as one of the more handsome men this island had ever seen. He was very popular with the ladies. I suppose your mom knew all about that."

Heather's smile waned. Could Jackie tell her anything about her mother and father, about the truth of her past?

"Do you have any memory of my mother, then? Jane? She would have been here in Bar Harbor in, oh, 1975, 1976... Before she and my father moved to Portland."

Or something like that, she thought. The timeline couldn't be trusted.

"Unfortunately not," Jackie admitted as she pressed her palms together. All the color drained from her cheeks. "Oh, gosh, honey, I can't imagine what you must feel. Lost your mother and father so long ago, and then back here, where all these ghosts live..."

Just then, Luke stepped out of the Eatery in his chef whites. His grey eyes latched onto Heather's. She felt again like a boat far out to sea with the first view of the lights from a lighthouse. He seemed to represent hope somehow.

"Hey there." Heather felt her own smile curve upward.

"Hey." He nodded, then gestured back toward the Eatery. "Nicole saw you walking up the steps. She forced me to prepare you a plate of food against my will. Maybe against yours, too."

Heather's stomach grumbled. It was true that she'd lost some kind of connection with her body. Hunger seemed like this other idea, something her anxious mind and her hunt for her past history shouldn't have had to bother with.

Heather and Luke sat at one of the two-seater tables near one of the large open windows, with its abrupt and almost overly dramatic view of Cadillac Mountain. The chef had made a fish risotto with a side salad. It simmered with flavor and smelled sinful. Heather slipped her fork along the edge of it, still feeling Luke's gaze upon her. In the back kitchen area, she could hear Nicole and the chef bickering.

"They're always at each other's throats," Luke finally broke the silence. "Nicole finally confessed to me last night that she wants to run the restaurant herself."

Heather looked at Luke with an arched eyebrow. Nicole had always been an incredible cook; she'd hosted some of the most splendid Christmas and Thanksgiving dinners, had invented multiple recipes, and looked at cooking, wine, and dessert-making as a kind of sacred practice. But she couldn't fully envision her as the head of a restaurant like the Eatery. Could she truly handle it?

"And to be honest, she has the passion this place really needs," Luke continued. "She took over a few days when the chef was out of town. Her meals were exquisite. She has a beautiful air in the kitchen, always a wonderful energy. It's infectious and easy to work alongside, you know, and since I'm the sous chef, in the middle of it all, I appreciate that."

Nicole had only briefly mentioned her dreams of becoming a chef. Heather hadn't considered, ever, that Nicole might not want to be the marketing and brand specialist she'd always been prior to her abrupt move to Bar Harbor. Why had Nicole been so closed off about her future plans? Did she feel embarrassed?

"And how about you?" Luke asked finally. "Your quest to find your family. Any answers yet?"

Heather shook her head. "My older sister checked out the records at the hospital our mother always said I was born at, over in Portland, but we could find anything. No such person was born there."

"Wow. That's really crazy and a little unsettling, to be honest."

"Tell me about it." Heather allowed her shoulders to drop. "I pored over my father's diaries again for some kind of clue. I even read over his short stories, his poems. But nothing tells the unique story of why the heck I was here in Bar Harbor without my supposed mother— or who my mother was, to begin with."

Luke chewed his risotto contemplatively. "Don't you hate that parents have to be just as fallible as the rest of us?"

Heather laughed in spite of herself. "I've always thought of my mother as a saint. I knew better than to think of my father like that. It's why we stayed away from Bar Harbor all these years. The story we always heard was that he left my mother and the three of us when we were too young to really understand, then came back to Bar Harbor where he owned a number of properties, including this place right here, and then eventually took his own life. Since my mother died when I was still quite young, she never got around to telling me the nitty-gritty details of, you know, why she fell in love with him in the first place or what he was actually like. When my sisters and I asked Aunt Tracy about him, she kind of made it out like he was this fool who was unworthy of my mother's love."

Nicole whipped out of the kitchen door again. Her cheeks were blotchy with rage after her argument with the chef. She lifted a hand to Heather and called, "How do you like the risotto?"

Heather nodded and tried a smile again. Still, food was the furthest thing from her mind. She had a sudden image of herself, Nicole, and Casey, all in their teenage years, huddled in Casey's bed as they'd watched *Sixteen Candles* together. She ached to return to those long-ago days— back when their fantasies surrounding their mother and father had been strong enough to lift their spirits.

"You haven't had a whole lot of fun since you arrived, have you?" Luke asked then.

Heather drew her eyes back to his beautiful grey ones. How could she describe that the concept of "fun" was a foreign word to her? She'd hardly laughed since Max's death. She had felt like a shell of a person.

"I'm going to take that as a no," Luke remarked, wiping his napkin across his lips. "What do you say we go out to a little popular tavern tonight? I know for a fact Nicole will be here, obsessing about every little detail about the menu she hates."

Heather's mind raced with sudden fear. What had she planned to do tonight, instead? Probably sit in a room by herself, read Adam's diaries over and over and obsess over who she was.

As though Luke could read her mind, he asked, "Unless you have something better to do?"

Heather grimaced. "No, that sounds good. I mean, that woman at the records office already said they're missing you down there. Rumor has it nobody can play darts like you."

Luke laughed outright as his cheeks burned pink with embarrassment. "No. Nobody can beat me at darts. That's for damn sure."

Heather set her jaw. "I take that as a challenge.

CHAPTER EIGHT

"HOW IS BAR HARBOR, MOM?" Bella's voice rang out of the phone, which Heather had propped up on the armoire in her room. Heather stood in her bra and panties— both dotted with holes, her feet spread shoulder-width apart, as she ogled her overly strange collection of clothes she'd managed to pack from Portland. Three black turtlenecks, a miniskirt, a strange lace dress with pockets, plus a pair of thigh-high boots? *Had she lost her mind?*

Well, yes. She had.

"Oh, it's good," Heather feigned a bright tone as she flung a green skirt out of the closet and onto her bed.

"Kristine and I hardly heard from you the past few days," Bella told her.

Heather could practically see that little wrinkle form between Bella's eyebrows. Bella and Kristine were identical twins— both with jet-black hair and sapphire eyes, like their mother. Often, people back in Portland had called them triplets, a fact that had embarrassed Bella and Kristine and pleased Heather to no end. "She's our MOM," they'd scoffed as teenagers.

"Oh, I've just thrown myself into life here, I guess," Heather tried. She pushed the button of the green skirt into its hole and gaped at her reflection in the armoire mirror. Green skirt, just a bra? The look made her look even more ragged than she felt.

"And how is Aunt Nicole? Did she tell you why she went to Bar Harbor without telling you guys?" Bella asked.

No. She hadn't. She'd mentioned briefly that her and Uncle Joe had built a rather beautiful friendship, yes; and she'd fallen head-over-heels for the Keating Inn and Acadia Eatery, but she hadn't fully described her journey from Portland all the way back to Bar Harbor, nor why she had decided to stay. Heck, she'd even told Luke she wanted to be a chef while hardly mentioning such a dream to her sisters.

"I think Aunt Nicole is going through a transition," Heather said finally as she slipped off her green dress.

"Aren't we all," Bella admitted with a tender laugh.

There was a brief moment of silence again. In the old days, Heather and Bella and Kristine had gabbed at one another with the vibrancy of gossip queens. Max had always said they reminded him of little Italian families in Rome who spoke continually over one another, without waiting for the other to stop. "How do you even keep track of what the others are saying?" he'd asked once, completely at a loss. "We're women. We can do more than two things at once," Heather had returned with a cheeky grin.

"Well, honey, I'd better get going," Heather finally said. "Wish you were here, as always. Tell your sister I love her to pieces."

"We love you to pieces, too," Bella said softly. Her voice seemed heavy with pain. "And we'll try to get out of the city soon to see you. Maybe when you head back to Portland?"

"Yes, maybe." Although even as she said it, Heather couldn't fully envision herself packing up her Prius again and returning to that empty, echoing house. Her own ghosts lurked there. At least here in Bar Harbor, the ghosts were of a far different variety. Perhaps that's all life was: a many-decade-long experiment, during which you had to choose which ghosts you reckoned with and which you ran away from.

Max was in every nook and cranny of that house in Portland. For a year, that had worked for her; she'd wanted to live in that dreamscape forever. But now, she felt herself full-on drowning.

After she hung up, Heather set to work on finalizing her look for the night ahead. She hadn't heard anything from Nicole regarding her plans with Luke. This probably meant that Luke had decided not to inform Nicole of their outing at the bar. It was for the best. Nicole had already mentioned that she didn't fully approve of Luke and that Heather should "watch out" for him.

But what was there to watch out for? Thus far, Luke had proven himself to be a worthy man to know. It had been eons since Heather had made a new friend. She would have been resistant to the idea of friendship had he not heard her blurt out that information about her mother. Maybe it was some kind of fate.

Even after everything, all the darkness of her life, Heather still had a small part of her that believed in magic. She was a writer; her books couldn't have thrived without it. Still, her version of magic seemed a little crumpled, a little used-up. She wasn't sure magic was something you could reuse and recycle.

Luke's massive pick-up truck hummed at the end of the

driveway. Heather gave herself a final up-down in the mirror. She'd gone with a little maroon dress, which hugged her curves and then ruffled down her thighs. A few years ago, Bella had actually tried to steal it, which made Heather believe it was something special. Her girls had sinfully good fashion taste.

Luke's eyes told her the full story of her dress when she jumped in the truck. For the first time in over a year, she felt like something special— no longer the weeping widow that sat in a huge hollow house on Portland hill. Heather clicked her seatbelt into place and flashed him a smile.

"So, you ready to get destroyed at darts?"

Luke clucked his tongue as he pulled away. "You talk a pretty big game for a children's author."

"What do you think children's authors are good for? We don't spend our whole lives staring at a screen and dreaming up little stories," she returned. Where had this snark been all this time? She grinned into it, grateful to find that part of herself again.

"I'll believe it when I see it," Luke told her.

He crept the truck into the back alley parking lot of a little dive bar. Heather laughed to herself as he grumbled about the lack of parking. It reminded her so much of Max, but not in a good or bad way. It just seemed like, no matter where you are or who you were with, men always found a reason to complain about the parking situation.

"Ah, here we go." Luke slid into the final spot, then turned off the engine.

"So weird that they're busy on a Friday," Heather quipped with a sneaky smile.

"That's about enough sarcasm out of you for the night," Luke returned.

They walked through the parking lot and then entered through a shadowed door in the back. As the screen door cranked open, sounds of the stereo buzzed through— an oldies' tune by REO Speedwagon. Luke's stance seemed to shift as he marched into the darkness. He had a real swagger like he owned the place. Heather wanted to tease him for it, but it was soon too loud in the bar for something like that. Luke's name was called from all corners.

There was a dark wooden bar off to the left, where three older gentlemen sat with large beers. An older woman in a miniskirt stood at the bar off to the right and called, "There he is, you son of a gun. Where have you been?"

Luke stepped up and hugged the older woman. "Busy! I told you, I got that new sous chef job."

"What the heck, Luke-y? You were meant to be a barfly with us till the end of time," one of the men at the bar said. "Ah, but we're so proud of you. We talk about going up to that Eatery all the time."

"I know you better than you know yourself, Benny. There's no way you're eating anything but bar snacks and burgers," Luke shot as he punched him playfully in the arm.

The woman from the records office stepped up from the pool table. She wore a light pink dress which shimmered, despite the dark light of the bar. Her breasts curved beautifully beneath the dress. Heather's stomach stretched with jealousy.

"Luke!" Monica cried. "I wondered if you might make an appearance after I nagged you the other day."

"It was you who nagged him?" the woman at the bar asked. "Good on you, Monica. Didn't know you had it in you."

Monica performed a little, playful curtsy, then batted her eyelashes. "I don't suppose I could buy you a drink in exchange for a game of pool?"

Luke's eyes curved toward Heather. Monica's gaze followed his as her smile fell.

"Or, we could all play together if you want to," Monica tried.

"Heather here already challenged me to a game of darts," Luke told her. "But maybe after?"

Before Monica could answer, Luke strutted over to the dart section and removed each dart, one by one. Heather nodded toward Monica and followed after him. She could feel the younger woman's disdain, and it somehow gave her power. When, in the history of the world, had the man gone for the sadder, older, lonelier option?

Ah, but he was just being nice.

Probably.

Luke disappeared back to the bar and arrived back with two light beers. He lifted them and said, "I hope these are okay?"

Heather laughed aloud. In truth, she hadn't drank a domestic beer out of a bottle in years. She had become something of a wine snob in recent years, especially as she had made more money, and she and Max had developed a taste for expensive flavors.

"I know. I'm a wine snob, too," Luke admitted then, as though he could read her mind. "But there's nothing like playing darts and drinking beer on a Friday night. It reminds me of being a teenager again."

It reminded Heather, too. She took a sip and allowed herself to fall back in line with those old memories— wild nights with Max, when they'd challenged local college students to vibrant dart games, which they had almost always won. Back then, they hadn't had more than a few pennies to rub together, but they'd always had time for one another, a game of darts, and a bottle of beer.

"Ladies first," Luke said then. He placed the dart in her outstretched palm and gave her a funny look.

"If you insist." Heather placed her bottle of beer on an empty table, aligned her body to the dart board, then whipped the dart forward. It landed just a half-inch or so to the right of the bullseye, which she was grateful for. After all, she'd talked a big game for someone who hadn't played in over fifteen years.

Luke whistled, clearly impressed. "I guess it's true. You're a force to be reckoned with."

They continued on. Their smack-talk took new heights as they played. At some points, Heather took the lead and then grew nervous and allowed Luke to inch forward. The rest of the bar-goers were rapt with attention, watching them. When it came down to the final points, Heather no longer felt like Heather Harvey Talbot, acclaimed children's fantasy writer. She felt only like a woman at a bar enjoying her time with this man— a man she now wanted to defeat at all costs.

When her final dart found the bullseye, she flung her arms into the air and howled with excitement. The rest of the bar (besides Monica) joined her in howling. Many clapped their hands.

"Oh, how the king has fallen!" the woman at the bar yelled out. She rushed toward Heather and wrapped her arms around her. "You're really something, my dear. Really something indeed."

Luke's cheeks were tinged red with embarrassment. Finally, he stuck out his hand for Heather to shake.

"Good sportsmanship. That's what I like to see," a man at the bar called out.

Heather's eyes locked with Luke's.

"You embarrassed me in my own environment. Can't say that's ever happened before," Luke admitted with a sneaky smile.

"Guess the next beer's on you, too," Heather returned, then took a swig of her beer.

"It's the least I can do."

They made their way to a table and sat. Heather could practically feel Monica's anger and urgent desire to be with Luke. Instead of taking it out on them, she spent a number of minutes at the juke box, picking ABBA songs and annoying the bar staff. Heather wondered if Luke and Monica had ever been an item but decided to keep the questions to herself.

"Thank you for bringing me here," Heather told him as she picked at the label on her bottle. "I haven't felt like myself. Not for a long time."

Luke nodded. "I understand what it's like to lose yourself. I know it's hard to get it back. Not saying I can help in any way. I can just offer distraction."

"Sometimes, distraction's the only thing," she replied.

Luke sniffed. He then nodded over toward the back area of the bar, where a number of framed photographs hung. "You know, your Uncle Joe was the first guy to take me here. He was a regular and a killer at darts, too."

There, toward the right end of the collection of photographs, hung a photo of Uncle Joe. In the photo, he was maybe mid-fifties, with a funny handlebar mustache.

"Did he lose a bet to grow that mustache?"

"Ha. I don't know. I wasn't around back then," Luke stated. "But he was a character. Eternally kind, giving and hilarious. He and Nicole were like two peas in a pod toward the end. I think he was grateful she gave him that chance."

Heather's cheeks burned with sorrow. She sipped her beer. "I regret that I missed all that."

"I'm sure you had your reasons for staying away. Everyone always does."

Here, Heather ached to ask Luke what he was staying away from and why he'd left the Midwest. But instead, Luke lifted his beer toward hers and gave her that ridiculously handsome smile.

"Here's to finding new reasons to go on," he offered.

"And here's to you getting better at darts. Someday," she teased.

They sipped and studied one another. One ABBA song flickered over to the next. For these moments, Heather was terribly grateful not to live in the chaos of her mind. Here, in the dark shadows of this dive bar, she was just a girl again. Secrets and sorrows and past horrors couldn't catch her. Not here.

CHAPTER NINE

IT WAS NEARLY midnight when Luke's wheels creaked along the end of the driveway. Heather had a funny jolt in her stomach, a memory of her high school boyfriend dropping her off at Aunt Tracy's several hours too late. Nicole and Casey had helped her slip into the back window, unnoticed. Now, the windows were warm, glowing orange, and vibrant; she could practically feel Nicole's waiting presence inside. Why did she feel she had to explain her absence? She was a forty-four-year-old woman.

"Thank you for the company," Heather told him.

"Thank you for being a worthy opponent," Luke returned. His eyes gleamed. "Let me know if you need any additional help on your search. I know how strange this all must be for you. But you're not alone."

Heather's throat tightened. "Why are you helping me?"

Luke lifted his eyes toward the house. On cue, Nicole stepped out in a dark grey robe and lifted a hand in greeting. Heather leaped out and remained in the curve of the open truck door.

"I just know what it's like to feel like you don't have answers," Luke told her. "Like the world is suddenly a dark place you can't trust."

"Can you trust the world?" Heather asked softly.

Luke shrugged. "I find new ways to convince myself I can trust the world all the time. Who knows if it's rational?"

Heather waved goodbye as Luke's truck snuck out the driveway. She then padded up toward the porch, just as a light rain began to fall. Nicole eased the door open for both of them without a word. When Heather stepped in, she began to ramble, coming up with reasons she'd been gone so long, reasons she hadn't told Nicole the truth.

"I just had to get out of the house," she began. "I just got all cooped up here and nervous about everything, and I wasn't sure how to deal with myself. I tried to talk to Bella on the phone, but it was awkward, and I didn't know what to say. And Nicole— when I look at you, I just…"

Here, she did fully look at her sister. Large caves swelled beneath Nicole's eyes. Her cheeks were blotchy. Had she been crying?

"Nicole. What's wrong?" Heather caught sight of a half-drunk bottle of wine in the living area. She shivered.

"Let's sit down. I have to tell you something," Nicole breathed.

Heather sat. She was reminded of performing such an action when the coast guard had come to her house with news of the accident out on the ocean. Why did they expect you to sit when they delivered such world-altering information? She supposed they didn't want you to faint.

Nicole poured them both glasses of wine and rubbed her palms together.

"If this is about Luke, I mean, nothing is going on," Heather said suddenly.

Nicole's eyes flickered. "I know. I mean." She pressed her fingers into her eyes, then dropped them. "Tonight was so crazy at the restaurant. And I got into fight after fight with the chef. I thought I was going to lose my mind."

Was this what this was all about? Heather sipped her wine and waited. She could be a listening ear. In fact, she welcomed it.

"Anyway, just after the dinner rush, I received a phone call from Uncle Joe's lawyer," she continued. "He's been around for ages and friendly with Uncle Joe and with Dad if you can believe it. Anyway, he's been in the process of figuring out exactly what we owe Brittany since she doesn't want anything to do with this property and in the process, he has discovered something strange."

Heather's lips tightened. She had absolutely no idea what to say.

"A long time ago, Dad was involved with a man at Snow Enterprises. The Snow family is the richest family in all of Bar Harbor and partial owner of the property we're sitting on right now. The lawyer found some of Dad's old work contracts with Snow, and, after reading through those, along with Dad's will, the lawyer learned that actually, Dad never did move to Portland. He was always here. Always working for Snow— until his death. But, as we know, Mom moved to Portland in 1976. The year I was born, and the year before you were."

Nicole's eyes were heavy with tears. She glanced away from her and sipped her wine.

"He then went on to tell me that he found a letter between our father and Uncle Joe in a file of Uncle Joe's old things— stuff Uncle Joe only just passed over to the lawyer in the past few months before his passing." Nicole continued. "In the letter, our father expresses a sincere doubt that— well..."

Heather's stomach tightened, and a sob escaped Nicole's lips.

"Nicole, it's okay. It's okay. If— if Jane isn't my mother, then..." Heather shrugged. "I'm starting to come to terms with that. Really."

But Nicole shook her head almost adamantly. "That's not it, Heather. It's bigger than that. In the letter, Dad doesn't think that you're actually his daughter, either. The lawyer called into question the idea that maybe you shouldn't be allowed the inheritance? That it should be between Casey and I only. But I told him that was ridiculous— that you're our biological sister, through and through. That..."

But through all this, a consistent ringing had came over Heather's ears. She no longer heard Nicole's words, could no longer make sense of any of this. She gaped at Nicole as Nicole sipped more of her wine, then fell back against the couch and shuddered.

Silence fell. Heather felt like someone who'd just landed on the moon and couldn't fully make sense of gravity or its lack thereof.

"I'm sorry..." Heather began finally.

Nicole blinked up.

"Did you just say that maybe, Dad isn't my Dad, either?"

Nicole closed her eyes tightly. "It's so stupid, Heather. We never should have dug through any of this. We should have left well enough alone."

Heather sat there in silence. Long ago, she'd written a children's book that had focused on the concept of telling the truth. In it, a bear lived alongside a hive of bees. The hive of bees had told him throughout his life that he was one of them, and they'd given him enough honey to sustain himself throughout his days. But one day, as he'd roamed through the woods, buzzing around, he had encountered a being who'd looked just like him— another bear. And he had asked his bee family, "Who am I?" The truth had freed him, but it had also hurt him a great deal. He missed his bee family when he returned to life with the bears, so much so that he went back frequently and told them stories about his great bear adventures.

"It's not your fault," Heather whispered.

Nicole pressed her palms against her thighs. "I just keep thinking that if the roles were reversed, it might destroy me. I can't imagine it. Going my whole life thinking Jane and Adam were my parents and then..." She snapped her fingers.

Heather shuddered. "Yeah. I know."

Nicole's eyes dropped. "I don't mean to rub it in. I just— I love you so much, Heather. So, so much. I—"

"I think we should do a DNA test, just to be sure," Heather blurted out.

Nicole's eyes were hollow. "We don't have to do that. We already know the version of the truth that we need. You're our sister, and nothing else matters."

"No. It matters. It really does," Heather told her softly. "I need to know the truth, Nicole. If this were you, you would too."

Heather stood and headed for the cabinet in the hallway, where she'd spotted a number of envelopes. In a monotone voice, she informed Nicole that she would put some strands of hair in the envelope and order a DNA test in the coming days.

"They're fast, now. It's like getting a tarot card reading or something," Heather said flatly. "Just, in this case, I guess, well..."

She removed several strands of hair and placed them gently within the envelope. In the living room, Nicole let out a strange sob. She then patted the side of the couch and whispered, "Sit with me for a while, Heather. Please."

But Heather couldn't sit. She couldn't peer into the pitying eyes of Nicole, who now looked at her as though she had three heads. She suddenly longed to be far, far away from this place, from its secrets, even as she felt suddenly that Bar Harbor was the seed from which her entire life had sprung.

Her parents, whoever they were, had been from here, it seemed like. She had to keep digging. She had to dismiss everything she had ever known and re-build.

CHAPTER TEN

LUKE WAS a perfectionist in the kitchen. Heather could feel his proud aura as he walked around the counter and instructed line cooks and prep cooks on the days' requirements. He spoke in low tones as he adjusted a line cook's way with the knife to ensure that he didn't embarrass him. He then disappeared into the walk-in freezer with the air of a soldier headed into battle. Apparently, there was a massive group headed into the Eatery for lunch. The chef had the afternoon off, which left the weight of it all upon Luke's shoulders.

When Luke stepped out into the bright light of the kitchen once more, his grey eyes found Heather's immediately. He lifted a large jar of something in greeting as his smile curved toward his ears. Heather's heart jumped.

"There she is. The woman who dragged my name through the mud at my favorite bar," he bantered. He placed the jar on the shining countertop and leaned against it with all the swagger of a handsome, flirtatious man. Slowly, his eyes squinted slightly as he took in the emotion across Heather's face. Obviously, something was very wrong.

"What is it?"

Heather glanced toward the listening line cooks and prep workers. "Can I speak to you? Just for a second."

Luke nodded and pointed toward the office, off to the side of the kitchen. They stepped within, where he shut the door. Heather scanned the small space, which included an old, framed photograph of Uncle Joe and her father on what looked to be a fishing trip. Adam had his arm swung around Joe's shoulder; he wore a bright yellow rain jacket and held a large fish aloft, with his fingers gripping the mouth of the giant, shining thing. Adam Keating looked so pleased with himself there, not the sort of man you might imagine would eventually take his own life.

"What's going on? More ghosts?" Luke asked, patiently leaning against the desk.

Heather splayed her hands on the top of the chair and informed Luke about the new information passed down from the lawyer. "I don't know what to make of any of this. I'm supposedly standing in a building that was passed down to me by a father who didn't even raise me. But ultimately, this family might not even be mine at all."

Luke clucked his tongue. "Wow, Heather. That's heavy."

"Nicole looked at me like I have three heads," Heather breathed. "I keep feeling like I should just jump in my car and drive back to Portland. But what then? Where's my family? I feel so, so lost."

Even more lost than after Max's death, she thought then. She wouldn't say it to Luke, though. He didn't need to shoulder her burden.

"I don't even know why I'm telling you this," Heather admitted. "I guess I just feel like, well..."

Luke placed a firm hand on her shoulder. "You shouldn't feel like you're alone in this."

Heather's throat tightened. "Okay." What else could she say? She wanted to toss her head onto his shoulder and weep.

"Is there anything else we can find out? You said the lawyer led Nicole to this information. Maybe we could read through the will for ourselves?"

Heather nodded. Luke's hand slowly swept down her upper arm. She trembled, if only for a moment. The intensity of the air between them made her feel like screaming.

"I can help you go over it after the lunch rush," he offered as he walked toward the door.

Without his hand on her arm, she felt suddenly empty and unbalanced. "Good luck out there."

"Sure. You know these Eatery folks. They eat like packs of dogs," Luke said, trying to lighten the mood. At the door, he bowed his head and then placed his hand on the doorknob. "You know, Nicole is probably just as surprised as you are. But there's no way in hell she'll let this get between you two. I hope you know that."

WHEN HEATHER TEXTED Nicole about the will, Nicole said that she'd already picked it up herself from the lawyer that morning but hadn't had time to go over it yet.

NICOLE: It's on the armoire in the living room. Feel free to dig through it.

NICOLE: We'll get to the bottom of this, sweetie.

NICOLE: At the end of the day, these are other people's decisions, from years and years ago. All we can do is be there for one another.

Heather perched at the desk in the living room, with her father's will before her. The radio hummed out news of the weather as though it was possible, in some other realm of thought, to care about such menial things. Max used to joke about the weather—how no matter where you were or who you spoke to, somebody always had something to say about it. Heather erupted from the chair and snapped the radio off.

Long ago, their Aunt Tracy had mentioned that Joseph and Adam Keating had owned a series of properties across Bar Harbor and Mount Desert Island. In her mind, Heather had made up a world in which her father had been sort of the king of Mount Desert Island. After his death, his three princesses had inherited his land.

But this had never gone through Heather. She'd received the monthly inheritance, as had been listed in the will, but she'd been too young back then to really dig into it herself. The money had never been a whole lot, but it had put her through college and helped with car down payments and bigger "adult" purchases when she'd been younger.

Now, she shifted back over the will and began to flip through, her eyes skimming the details.

LAST WILL AND TESTAMENT OF ADAM KEATING

I, Adam Keating, a resident of and domiciled in Bar Harbor, Maine, and a citizen of the United States of America, declare this to be my last will and hereby revoke all wills and codicils heretofore made by me, either jointly or severally.

Heather shuttered at the language. As a children's book writer, she tried her darnedest to avoid such highfalutin language. Still, this was the tradition of the law.

After the initial statement, the will moved toward three declarations— one that stated Adam Keating was of sound mind and that the will was a reflection of his wishes "without undue influence or duress."

The second declaration stated that, at the time of the writing, Adam Keating wasn't married to anyone. This was curious to Heather, as she hadn't known that her parents, or the people known as Adam and Jane, had ever officially divorced.

The third declaration stated:

C. I hereby declare that I have the following children:

Casey Harvey, born May 22, 1974

Nicole Harvey, born April 14, 1976

Heather Harvey, born February 25, 1977

Heather's spine quaked as she sat there, starting at the words before her. She continued to read, just as her phone blared with Luke's name across it. She snapped the phone to her ear.

"Hey, Luke."

"I've been knocking on your door for ages," Luke said. She could feel the smile behind his voice.

"Oh gosh. I'm in another world," she told him. She then swept out toward the foyer with the phone still pressed to her ear. She spotted Luke through the little window, where he waved.

"There you are," he said into the phone.

Heather opened the door and beamed at him. His hat glittered with the rain that had begun without her noticing.

"Come in! Come in," she told him hurriedly. "How was lunch?"

"Another storm," Luke told her. "I nearly lost my mind fourteen times, but we managed to get through it."

Heather shifted around him to close the door. Just before she turned back, she had a strange flashing image of a previous version of herself, greeting Max after his long weeks at sea. How excited she'd been to open the door to welcome him home. This wasn't that; it was merely a cousin to that emotion. Still, it was nice to feel it again.

Luke stepped toward the large desk, where a smattering of papers created a kind of harried art project. He placed his large hands on his hips and exhaled.

"I see you're up to your ears in will and testaments," he stated, glancing around.

Heather let out an exasperated laugh. "I was just digging into the addendums. It seems like some things changed close to the end of his life. Here, take a look."

Luke hovered over her as Heather sat in the chair. She ruffled toward the end, where her finger scanned across the addendums. "Ah! Look."

Luke read aloud. "The following properties will be left to my daughters, Casey, Nicole, and Heather. My one-half of the Keating

Inn and Acadia Eatery, along with the office building I built alongside an investor, possibly part-owner, Snow Enterprises."

"Snow Enterprises?" Nicole said my dad worked with them. That they're the richest family in Bar Harbor."

Luke's face grew shadowed. "I'm pretty sure your Uncle Joe worked with them, too."

"You don't sound thrilled about that."

Luke grumbled inwardly. "Darwin Snow isn't around anymore, so I never met the guy. I've just heard stories at the bar about his... shall we say, cruelty regarding his business operations. Most everyone else in Bar Harbor is incredibly kind and loyal and considerate. The kinds of people who would bend over backward for you just to make sure you have a second cup of coffee. Not so with the Snow family. They still own much of the land across Bar Harbor and the surrounding areas, but old Darwin's dead now."

"Hmm. If Darwin Snow is dead, who operates Snow Enterprises?"

"The Snow brothers," Luke offered. "Elijah and Evan. Neither of them are the type of guys I'd personally like to have a beer with if you catch my drift."

"Drift caught," Heather affirmed. She continued to gaze at this clue in the will, this strange other element of her father's life. "He built the office himself?"

"Your Uncle Joe told me your dad was also a trained carpenter. That's how he made money before they started to buy up all these old properties. I think something happened along the way. Something that made Snow Enterprise either loan them money or invest in their property."

"Then I think we have to talk to the Snow brothers," Heather said suddenly.

Luke's gaze affirmed something: that she was walking into territory she couldn't possibly understand. Still, she didn't want anything else for herself. She was a stranger, even unto herself.

"Are you going to drive? Or should I?" Luke asked then.

Heather stood and collected the papers, drawing them against her chest. "You don't have to help me, you know."

Luke shrugged. "It's not like there's anything else going on in our little sleepy coastal town of Bar Harbor. You're the one with the mysterious past. Everyone else is preparing for another night of pool, darts, and light beer."

Heather sighed. "I'd give anything for that."

Luke's eyes reflected something else: a bit of his own mystery, maybe. Heather lifted her chin as questions buzzed beneath the surface between them. But before she could ask, Luke lifted his keys from his pocket and tossed them into the air.

"Like I said, Evan Snow isn't my top-pick for Man of the Year," he told her. "If we're lucky, we can interrupt his lunch and really annoy him."

CHAPTER ELEVEN

THE AIR in Luke's truck sizzled with a mix of excitement and adventure. Rain splattered across the windowpane as they drove off from the Keating House, taking the driveway that led past the Keating Inn. Luke pointed toward a large parking spot in the gravel, where two large marks swept into the ground.

"That's where your Uncle Joe used to park his truck," he explained somberly. "For years and years. Nobody dares park there now that he's gone."

Heather's heart jumped at this. "Where is the truck now?"

"He left it to an old friend of his," Luke explained. "Marvin."

Heather opened her lips with sudden excitement, even as Luke explained, "But Marvin never knew your dad. He came around years later."

"You knew what I would ask even before I asked it? Who's the real detective here," Heather asked.

Luke banged his fist against his chest, faking his pride. "You know me. I'm a regular Sherlock."

At that moment, Heather's phone blared with news from the outside world. Bella's name appeared: a reminder that Heather hadn't exactly been Mother of the Year in terms of communication lately.

"You should take that," Luke advised. "The drive to the Snow mansion isn't a quick one. They tucked themselves as far away from the other Bar Harbor idiots as they could. Their word for us, not mine."

"Are you serious? That's what they call the people of this community?" Heather was infuriated by the comment.

"Of course," Luke confirmed. "You don't want to hear all my boring drivel. I'm about used up in the conversation department."

Heather chuckled. "I don't think that's true for a minute." Still, she answered the phone and soon heard both of her twins' voices. The sound of both of them together lightened her heart. Since they were identical twins, many assumed their voices were similar, but as their mother, Heather knew their differences in her soul. Bella's was lighter, airier, while Kristine's told a more serious story. This translated to their personalities, as well. Kristine was more artistic like her mother; Bella planned to take on the medical world and become a nurse.

"Mom!" Bella cried.

"There she is. The mystery woman," Kristine added.

"Hi, girls." Heather's eyes darted toward Luke. What did he think of her having daughters? What did he think of children at all? "How is everything?"

The twins held the silence for a moment.

Finally, Bella said, "We want to come to see you."

"Oh, girls. I don't know if that's necessary." In truth, Heather just couldn't comprehend explaining the depths of all this chaos. How could she possibly be a mother to her girls if she didn't know who she was any longer?

"Necessary? You don't think it's necessary to see your two only children?" Kristine asked half-jokingly.

Heather's nostrils flared as the rain ramped up. She heaved a sigh, then said, "What were you thinking of doing?" If they had a plan, maybe she could somehow hide her quest. Maybe they could do regular mother-daughter things. Hike the mountains. Eat in some of the ridiculously delicious seafood restaurants. Engage in the world around them in some way that didn't involve Heather crying in her bed.

"We already took the next week off," Kristine explained.

"Girls, you should have told me..." Heather said.

"See? She doesn't want us," Bella teased.

"That's not it," Heather stated.

"Are you really so busy in Bar Harbor?" Kristine asked.

"No. I mean. No." Heather wanted to lie and say she was knee-deep in plotting a new book, but she bit hard on her tongue just before. "I'll book the flights when I get home. Okay?"

Bella whooped. Kristine heaved a sigh and said, "Thank goodness. I need some time away from this place."

"This place? You make it sound like New York is a prison," Heather interjected.

"Kristine just got dumped," Bella countered.

Heather's lips curved upward. Kristine gasped and said, "Bella! Why did you tell her that?"

"Darling, it's okay. We've all been dumped before," Heather said.

Luke glanced her way. The red light above them flashed to green, and he shifted the truck forward as his face played out a little laughter.

"The great Kristine Talbot has never been dumped," Bella jested.

"I'm going to kill you, Bell," Kristine muttered.

"Suffice it to say, we need ice cream, hikes, and plenty of wine," Heather said finally. "I'll send you the flight info when I have it, okay?"

They said their goodbyes and their "see you later's" and then jumped off the phone. Heather burst into a silly laugh and tossed her head back.

"What was all that about all of us being dumped before?" Luke asked, still with that crooked grin across his face.

"One of my twins got dumped," Heather explained as she swiped a tear from her cheek. "Just reminds me of being a teenager. When you feel like your whole life is attached to this stupid boy, you know, just before he breaks your heart for the head cheerleader or something. The girls are twenty-two now, but you know how things go these days. People don't marry as early as they used to. They're bound for a few more years of heartache before they find their forever person."

"And you'll be there to pick up the pieces of their hearts along the way," Luke countered.

Heather laughed again. "They've spent the past year watching me crumble after their father..." She trailed off as her lips quivered —what a strange mix of emotions this all was. "I thought I didn't want them here in the midst of all this. But Nicole and I are sending in the DNA test results, and the wait will be hellish. I think the girls will be a welcome distraction."

"I hope you'll let me meet them," Luke said softly.

Heather's heart banged hard against her ribcage.

"I mean, if you stop by the Acadia Eatery, I can cook something up for them," Luke hurriedly added. "I'm one of the best chefs in Bar Harbor. Don't tell your sister I said that." He winked as silence fell between them.

"It's just so strange to not know anything or the real truth about my family and then have the girls come up in the middle of all of it," Heather said finally. "But I guess a whole lot of parenting is not knowing anything at all and figuring it out along the way."

"Well said," Luke concurred. "Never been a parent myself. It looks messy."

Messy. That was a word for it. Heather thought back to that diary she'd found of her father's, in which he talked about the struggles of parenting Casey. That had only been his first child. What had happened next?

The Snow Mansion was an elaborate, stone-built home from the mid-1900s, with a cast-iron gate nearly ten feet high around the grounds. The grass was so green it almost looked like fake turf, as though it had never had to handle the weight of a human foot. The grounds themselves seemed like royal gardens anywhere else. Rose petals of many shades caught the grey light perfectly; shrubs had been manicured into elaborate shapes.

"What is this? The Secret Garden or something?" Heather muttered.

"Not so secret," Luke shot out as he eased the truck toward the intercom near the fence.

"I never imagined it would be like breaking into a castle," Heather commented while her eyes took in the sight before her.

"Good afternoon," a man's voice sounded from the intercom. "How may I be of service to you today?"

"Hi there," Luke said. "Henry, isn't it?"

The man sputtered into the intercom. "Is that Luke?"

Luke flashed his eyes toward Heather, who nodded, impressed.

"Sure is," Luke replied. "Haven't seen you down at the bar lately. I guess old Snow has you running wild with tasks. What was it you said you are now? The house butler?"

Henry's voice lowered. "It's quite an undertaking, to be honest with you. I'm too exhausted for my pint at the end of the day."

"Phew. Can't imagine."

Heather weaved her arms across her chest. Where was this going?

"Anyway. You must know about Old Snow's operations with the Keating brothers," Luke continued. "I have one of the daughters of the Keating brothers here. She'd like to speak with Evan. Not sure if you can arrange that?"

Henry grumbled into the mic. "Luke, I don't know. I just started this job. I don't know that I can really strong-arm Mr. Snow into a meeting like that."

Heather whispered then, "Tell him about the will."

Luke nodded hurriedly. "One of the daughters of Adam Keating spotted an addendum in the will regarding a piece of property that should belong to her and the rest of his children.

Maybe you could mention that to Mr. Snow? Otherwise, you know we could always track down a lawyer and come on back."

Henry's voice darkened. "I'll be right back."

In the silence that followed, Luke smashed his hands across the steering wheel and whooped. Heather laughed brightly.

"That was sinister, Luke."

"Sinister?" Luke's smile faltered the slightest bit.

"But also one of the coolest things I've ever witnessed in my life. You intimidated him."

Luke shrugged playfully. "I never liked Henry that much. He was always too snooty for his own good. He belongs to the Snow people now— and anyone with any self-respect wouldn't go near Snow Enterprises these days."

"Huh." Heather's mind raced with intrigue.

"Not to say your father and uncle made a mistake in working with them. I think Snow Enterprises was brand-new back then. They came to Bar Harbor with dreams of taking over. And boy, did they take over. Ah. Look! It worked."

The cast-iron fence began to creak open, apparently automated by a button somewhere on the inside. Luke's tires creaked against the pavement as they drove through the gates.

"I don't think they've ever had the likes of this truck on these grounds," Luke said. "Nothing short of Porsches and Lamborghinis."

"Maybe you should run off the driveway just the slightest bit. The grass won't know what hit it," Heather teased.

"I think if I did that, Evan Snow would have me thrown in jail," Luke told her as he cut the engine.

That moment, a man in a little black suit appeared in the

doorway. He had a small mustache and a bald head, and his ears stuck out on either side of his egg-shaped head, like a child's.

"That's Henry," Luke muttered. "Gosh, he's really gone all out with the butler thing, I guess."

Henry beckoned for them to enter. Luke and Heather stepped out of the truck. Heather adjusted her cardigan as her stomach sizzled with anxiety. Whoever these people were, the way they flaunted their wealth didn't appeal to her. She'd always felt like the odd woman out at various publishing functions around people who wore their wealth in this way. They'd always looked at her like she had a third head, *"What are you doing here? You don't belong."*

"Hi there, Henry," Luke greeted casually.

"Mr. Snow will see you in his office, but he doesn't have much time," Henry informed them curtly.

"Perfect. We don't have much time for him, either," Luke informed him.

Heather grimaced. Fear rushed over her. Why had her father been involved with these people? And if they actually had answers for her, would she actually like what she found?

CHAPTER TWELVE

EVAN SNOW WAS MUCH MORE handsome than he should have been allowed. He sat upon an overly tall chair at the head of an antique desk with his large hands folded across the glow of the wood. He was certainly tall, with shaggy black hair and sapphire eyes. His cheekbones were high and jagged, like a Northern European's, and even the air's perfume reeked of wealth. Over the desk hung a portrait of a middle-aged man upon a horse. Heather had to assume this was Darwin Snow.

"Good afternoon," Evan said. He stood and gave Heather and Luke firm handshakes. He blinked at Heather with the slightest bit of curiosity. "Before your sister's arrival a few months back, I never imagined I'd catch sight of a Keating girl."

Heather longed to articulate that, in fact, she'd never been called a Keating girl in her memory. Always a Harvey girl, her mother's maiden name. She imagined that sort of argument wouldn't help her cause, though.

"Hello, Mr. Snow. Thank you for meeting me on such short notice." Heather settled into the chair across from him and used the tone of voice she normally reserved for those higher-ups in the publishing world. She could feel Luke's surprise at the sound of it; she'd been eternally herself with him. This other version was the version that got things done.

"My butler mentioned something about your father's will."

It seemed he wanted to cut straight to the chase.

"Yes. I didn't know that my father had left his daughters anything in relation to your estate," Heather continued.

"And in fact, I think our legal team could argue that anything upon our property never belonged to your father at all," Mr. Snow countered.

Heather's throat tightened. What did she care about his property? All she wanted was more information about her father.

"I don't mean to cause you any trouble, Mr. Snow," she continued. "It's only that my father left very, very few documents behind. There are many holes in his story, holes I'm attempting to explore."

"I suppose when one exits the world the way Adam Keating did, one leaves many questions," Evan replied coldly.

Heather almost wanted to laugh at how sinister this man was. Clearly, it was an act— proof of a man who'd struggled to feel much love in the world.

"Yes. You can imagine that it's been a struggle for me," Heather said. "Although I imagine, in the same breath, you wonder why you should care. You shouldn't. My only question to you is this: that office that belonged to my father must have had a number of his things within it, including documents that would be of great interest to me."

Evan shifted his weight. "You must know how long ago that was."

"I do."

Why was he so resistant? Heather furrowed her brow. She wished her gaze could penetrate this horrible man's cranium and dig into what lurked behind.

"As far as I know, we here at Snow Enterprises have nothing at all that belonged to Adam Keating," Evan articulated.

"Would you mind going over your things a second time?" Heather asked. "I know it must be an annoying task, but it's really one that I would appreciate."

Evan's cheek twitched. "As I've already said, we have none of your belongings whatsoever. I'm grateful, in the meantime, for your comprehension that the office that once belonged to your father is on our property and none of your concern."

Heather arched an eyebrow. Was this suddenly a dead-end? She glanced toward Luke, who sat with glittering eyes. Probably, he had about a million insults he wanted to fling toward Evan. She was grateful he held back his spitfire ways.

Evan suddenly stood and adjusted the button on his suit jacket. "Now, if you'll excuse me, I have a number of things to attend to," he said. "A life at Snow Enterprises is a busy one."

Heather stood on quivering legs. She felt herself shake Evan's hand again. There was the creak of the door as Henry beckoned them back out through the main entrance. In a flash, she felt herself again in Luke's front seat as he directed the truck away from the mansion.

"That asshole," Luke muttered.

Heather sputtered. "If he doesn't have anything, then he doesn't have anything. I guess I have to believe him."

"He still doesn't have to treat you like a piece of garbage," Luke continued. "That's the thing with these Snow guys. They think they own the whole town. Think they can say whatever they want and get away with it."

"He has all the power here. If he does find it within himself to look through some old boxes, he really might find my father's things," Heather breathed. "It frustrates me to no end."

"You can't rely on the kindness of a Snow," Luke stated. "It's just the way they are."

Heather paused for a moment. Clouds overhead seemed to darken and thicken, swirling menacingly. "I'm glad I can rely on the kindness of you, Luke. Really. Thank you for coming here with me today." She reached across the space between them with a sudden desire to touch his hand.

But at that moment, a car pulled out in front of Luke, and he slammed on the brake in a hurry. They narrowly missed the bumper of the car as he muttered, "Gosh. I didn't know they gave licenses to complete idiots."

Heather laughed and returned her hand to her thigh. What had she been thinking? He didn't owe her anything— nothing of his emotional self, nothing of his honesty. If anything, she was just grateful to have a friend who didn't look at her the way so many had the past year: like a widow, a woman who would never find solid ground again.

THAT NIGHT, Heather poured herself and Nicole glasses of pinot noir, curled up on the back porch, and dialed Casey to tell her the recent findings. Casey listened in rapt attention and then muttered, "What a jerk," about Evan Snow.

"I guess I can see it from his perspective," Heather admitted. "Why should he care about some woman's quest to find her parentage?"

"Yeah, but still. It sounds like Dad and Uncle Joe worked tirelessly for these people," Nicole interjected. "Uncle Joe mentioned several times that they weren't exactly kind, especially toward the end, when Dad really struggled with his mental health. The least they could do right now is, I don't know, just check to see if a few boxes might have belonged to Dad."

Casey heaved a sigh. On video chat, she sipped her own glass of wine. She looked overly tired. Heather's heart felt gripped with sorrow. She wished Casey was there with them. She needed her big sister.

"Why don't you come over to see us?" Heather finally asked.

"I don't know," Casey returned.

"What don't you know?" Heather asked.

Casey bit hard on her lower lip. "It's just that... well..."

But Heather could already see it, reflected back in Casey's eyes. This situation was messy. It was a dark pit that Casey hadn't allowed herself to gaze into for essentially her entire life. After a pause, Casey admitted, "I just don't know why we should care about Dad at all, you know? He wanted nothing to do with us. And at the end of the day, Heath, you grew up with us. It was always you, me, and Nicole against the world. Remember?"

Heather's heart felt bruised. How could she explain that it wasn't so simple for her any longer?

"Jane is your mother, Casey," Heather said softly. "But if she's not mine, then I'd like to know who is."

Casey's eyes filled with tears. "But Heather, Mom died so long ago, too. You're dealing with ghosts. Why don't you look at what's really in front of you? Me and Nicole and your daughters..."

Heather felt shadowed with shame. "I just can't accept the way things are if they're not the full truth. I need this, Casey. I'm sorry to say that, but I do."

Casey nodded. There was a strange moment of silence before she whispered, "Okay. I guess I have to respect that." She then admitted to wanting to get off the phone to tend to some things around the house.

When she was finally gone, Nicole placed a hand over Heather's and said, "We'll get to the bottom of this. Somebody around here has to know the truth."

Heather's lower lip quivered. "I feel like such a fool for not coming here before Uncle Joe died."

Nicole shook her head. "Don't beat yourself up about it. Life happened the way it happened. None of it was ideal. It's like I kept asking myself after Michael left. What was it all for? What did it mean? I don't even know if I have an answer for it. Not yet. But suffice it to say, as I dig into those emotions, I'm trying my darnedest to push forward and seek something. Somehow, I've found meaning in operating the Keating Inn and Acadia Eatery. I never in a million years expected that for myself."

Heather gripped her sister's hand harder. "There's a glow about you I haven't seen in years, Nic. It gives me hope for a brighter tomorrow for myself. Maybe that's silly to say."

"No, not at all. The only silly thing is thinking that just because these people in the past made certain choices and mistakes means that we must change anything about the here and now. I understand wanting to know the truth. But I won't allow you to let yourself be buried in it. Is that clear?"

Heather smiled through her tears. "Crystal clear. I promise you that."

CHAPTER THIRTEEN

THE BAR HARBOR AIRPORT was a rinky-dink little place, barely an airport at all. Heather gripped the steering wheel of her Prius as her eyes scanned left and right, hunting for some sign of her daughters. Their plane had landed twenty minutes earlier, and upon their arrival, her heart had filled with excitement, pumping faster and brighter than it had in weeks. Bella and Kristine would remind her what it meant to be herself; they would give her the strength to nurture and laugh and remember the old version of Heather, the one who had taken life by the horns.

Bella and Kristine had had one single phase of dressing alike, back when they'd been eight or nine and very into the idea of the Olsen twins. Back then, they had donned bright pink leotards and erupted around Max and Heather's Portland house, practicing whatever new form of ballet they'd invented that day. Max had joked at the time, "Why didn't we have just one boy? Someone I could play catch with in the backyard?" This had resulted in his two little ballerinas rushing into the backyard and demanding to play baseball in their leotards. The three of them had come back into the house, exhausted, covered in glitter, somehow, and eager to jump around all the more. After Max had taught them how to throw, the girls had instructed him on their ballet moves, and Heather had watched on the old white couch in the living room as they'd performed for her.

Stop, her mind told her now. *Stop before you run yourself wild with tears.*

But here the girls were: dressed entirely differently, both to highlight their very different personalities. Kristine was the artistic one, with flowing dresses and thick black boots. Bella wore a simple pair of jeans, wider at the legs, as was the new style, with a V-neck white t-shirt. Both had jet-black hair, like their mother, and it flowed beautifully down their backs, catching the glittering light that came in through the smattering of clouds on high.

Heather had never seen a more beautiful pair. She erupted from her car and waved a hand to greet them. Bella rolled her eyes as they approached and said, "You thought we wouldn't see you? You're basically the only car."

"Nice to see you too," Heather quipped. She jumped onto the sidewalk as the three of them fell into a ridiculous hug. Wave after wave of emotion fell over her. Even the way they smelled was the same— a reminder of long-lost days when they had all lived together under one roof, with Max Talbot, the one who'd gotten away for good.

"Wow. Look at this place," Bella commented from the front seat as Heather eased them toward the town, which formed brightly across Frenchman Bay in a collection of unique coastal houses and buildings.

"It's certainly not New York," Heather affirmed, giving her daughter a sideway glance.

"Thank goodness," Kristine added from the back seat.

"It's a really unique little place," Heather said, adjusting herself in her seat. It felt strange to drive, as she'd hardly done anything but walk around or else let Luke drive her. Her daughters couldn't sense that off of her, she supposed. They just saw what they needed to see: their mother, a source of comfort. She could be that.

"So sweet of you girls to want to visit me here," Heather said as Bella flickered through the radio stations. "Your employers are okay with it?"

"We have a number of clients flirting with us right now, but we just closed out a few big projects," Kristine explained. She worked part-time as an interior designer for a few high-paying Manhattan clients while she obtained her creative writing degree. "It was a perfect time for me."

"And I thought if I pushed myself through another shift at the hospital, I might have a nervous breakdown." Bella articulated.

Heather felt a stab of fear at the comment.

"Don't freak Mom out," Kristine warned her sister.

"Sorry, Mom," Bella offered. "I was mostly kidding, anyway."

Okay, so maybe her kids understood her inner emotional life better than she'd thought. They were certainly smarter than their own good.

It was just past twelve when they reached the Keating House at the edge of the property. Bella and Kristine were both appreciative of the gorgeous house. "It really looks like something from a storybook," Bella gushed.

Nicole and Heather had prepared one of the large guest bedrooms upstairs for Kristine and Bella to share. Heather watched from the doorway as her daughters gathered their things atop the bed and adjusted their makeup in the mirror.

"I hope it's okay that you girls share a room?" Heather asked.

Bella and Kristine side-eyed each other, then burst into laughter.

"Kristine won't stop staying at my place," Bella told her with a funny smile. "She booty-calls me and asks if she can come over."

"Don't tell Mom all my secrets!"

Bella shrugged as Kristine blushed.

"I just didn't want to be alone after Allen broke things off." Kristine dabbed at her bottom lip while she looked at herself in the mirror.

"That's another thing," Bella continued. "His name was Allen. Have you ever cried over a guy named Allen?"

Heather sniggered as Kristine playfully smacked Bella across the arm. "As I already told you on the plane, I'm coming to terms with the fact that I made a really big mistake in dating him, okay? Is that enough for you?"

"I don't think so. It'll never be enough," Bella teased.

BELLA AND KRISTINE'S energy and warmth made Heather feel as though she floated through time. She donned a bright mustard-yellow dress and met her daughters in the foyer, where they suggested grabbing something to eat before exploring Bar Harbor. Heather thought nothing of it when she suggested they head up to the Eatery. After all, the Eatery was one-third hers, according to Adam Keating's last will and testament. She'd hidden all that paperwork away prior to Bella and Kristine's arrival and had told Nicole to make no mention of the DNA test. "I just want a normal week with my girls. As normal as normal can be after everything else," she'd instructed her sister.

But the moment she, Bella, and Kristine entered the Eatery, Luke stepped into the dining area in his chef whites (which made him look all the more handsome) and brought with him a rush of fears and innermost secrets. He looked at her with curiosity and then beamed at Bella and Kristine as he greeted them.

"You must be Heather's daughters," he smiled. "We've been excited about your arrival. Who knows what trouble you three will get into."

Bella turned her gaze toward Heather. Her eyes were heavy with intrigue.

To combat this, Heather made her tone flatter than normal. She couldn't appear to flirt with this man.

"They're already up to no good, I'm sure." Heather locked eyes with Luke and flashed him a half-smile.

"But mostly, we're starving," Kristine jumped in then.

Luke laughed. "I can help you with that."

"But who are you?" Bella asked.

"Oh, right. I'm Luke. I've worked here at the Eatery for a few years, first with your Great-Uncle Joe and now with your Aunt Nicole. I just moved up to sous chef ranking."

"Ah. Well, you should know, we have a very refined palate," Kristine teased.

"Yes. We're not usually impressed," Bella offered.

Heather scoffed. "I'll have you know that these girls grew up on chicken fingers and tater tots. Nothing refined about their palates. No matter how long they live in New York City..." She rolled her eyes.

The three Talbot ladies sat together at a table near the window. Bella lifted her phone to try to catch Cadillac Mountain perfectly with her camera. With each snap, she whispered, "You really can't get a good photo of it, can you? It's like trying to catch a sunset."

The server appeared with a large basket of freshly-baked bread. The bread was sinful, buttery and cloud-like, and both Bella and Kristine moaned as they tore into it.

"I thought we said no bread till Christmas?" Bella said as she lifted another piece from the basket.

"Pfft. Those are city rules. Bar Harbor doesn't apply," Kristine insisted.

Luke served them a blissful meal— a cheesy ravioli with eggplant, an enormous Greek salad, and a dessert of cheesecake. Throughout, Luke continued to pester them with questions, asking them what they thought of the meal.

"It's soooo good," Bella declared as she closed her eyes. "Seriously, you could give any Manhattan chef a run for his money."

Luke's smile was electric. That moment, Nicole stepped toward the table to greet her nieces with hugs and cheek kisses. "I'm so sorry I can't step away to hang out today. It seems like I'm putting out a million little fires across the inn and Eatery."

"I hope they're not literal fires," Kristine said.

"Not yet, anyway," Nicole affirmed. "What is your plan for the afternoon?"

Bella and Kristine turned to look at Heather as though Heather had some kind of grand scheme. In reality, she'd hardly ever envisioned them making it there; now that they were, she was at a loss. All she wanted to do was roam the beaches and mountains with them, listen to them chatter and laugh, and fall into the old version of herself. The version which had been happy. The version who'd had it all.

"I could take you girls out on my boat if you like," Luke suggested suddenly.

Bella and Kristine's eyes brightened.

"Oh my gosh. That sounds beautiful," Bella replied as she looked to her sister and then her mother.

"You just want good photos for your social media," Kristine argued.

Bella rolled her eyes. "Not everything is about social media, Kris. I like to live, too, you know."

"That sounds like a beautiful afternoon," Nicole said.

"I just have to wrap up a few things in the kitchen; then I can drive us down to the harbor," Luke said. Already, he'd begun to unbutton his chef's whites. "If you girls want to change or grab your suits or something, I can meet you at the house in forty-five minutes?"

A cloud of joyousness ballooned over their table. All the while, Heather's mind burrowed into darkness. The water? The same water that had taken her Max from the world forever? Could she feasibly get onto a boat without having some kind of panic attack?

She closed her eyes, then sipped a bit of her water. Kristine and Bella began to argue over who would wear "the green dress," which was apparently a dress they'd purchased together with the idea of sharing it. If Heather had been on earth at that moment, she might have asked how they'd ever found a dress that they'd agreed upon. All she could do just then was inhale, exhale. Focus. Live in the here and now.

A kind man wanted to spend time with her and her daughters.

It was a beautiful day at the beginning of September.

She'd hardly done anything but pore over documents and dig into family secrets since her arrival.

She needed to live again. She needed to feel again.

She had to be strong in the face of this. It was just a sailboat. It was just Frenchman Bay. Nothing could hurt them again.

But wasn't that optimism what had gotten her in trouble in the first place?

Back at the house, she watched as first Bella and then Kristine donned the green dress with its unique little white flowers. Apparently, it had been made in the sixties and was something of an iconic piece, which was why they hadn't been able to find a second. Ultimately, the girls decided they didn't want to muss it with a sailing expedition and instead donned other summery dresses, little jean jackets, and tennis shoes, which Luke had told them were appropriate to get a better grip on the sailboat floor.

As Bella slipped a pair of earrings into her ears, she studied her mother. "He's cute," she finally said.

Heather's stomach tightened. "Who?"

"You know who."

Heather grimaced. "Luke's just a friend. He's been very welcoming since I arrived."

"Yeah? I wonder why," Bella said, giving her a sneaky smile.

It was the same sneaky smile Max used to give Heather back in the old days. He had used it when he'd tried to hide that he had planned a surprise birthday party for her thirtieth; he'd used it when he had eaten all the leftovers in the fridge.

She couldn't love anyone else but him. Never in a million years.

"Shall we head down?" Kristine called. "I think I just heard Luke's truck. Oh wow. It's massive. Is he compensating for something?"

"Kristine..." Heather said, grateful, suddenly, for the desire to laugh. She grabbed her baseball hat and snuck it over her head, suddenly eager for the hours ahead. Adventure was out there, if you were only brave enough to seek it.

CHAPTER FOURTEEN

LUKE'S BOAT was called *Matilda*. The name was painted across the side in beautiful calligraphy. The white hull crept up across the shimmering waves as Luke ducked up over it, checking various ropes with a sure sense of himself, of his skill. He looked more muscular than normal, tanned from many days on the water, and his smile was bright and handsome as Heather and her daughters watched on.

"You sure you know what you're doing?" Bella called.

Luke laughed. "I never know what I'm doing."

"That's reassuring," Kristine added.

He'd packed a little picnic: two bottles of champagne, berries, and cream. Bella and Kristine hopped onto the boat without pause as Heather remained on the creaking dock. She blinked out toward the horizon line, so bright and hopeful beneath the Northeastern sun. Could she convince herself to board?

"I don't think Allen could have done this," Bella said to Kristine with another ironic grin.

"Can you just lay off the Allen convo for a minute?" Kristine demanded.

Bella shrugged as Luke laughed.

"Do I even want to know?" he asked.

"No. You don't want to know Allen," Bella affirmed. "He wore more cologne than all three of us combined. You could smell him all the way from A Avenue— but he lived in Brooklyn!"

Luke stepped toward the dock and stretched out his palm for Heather to take. He wanted to be her support, both morally and physically. She placed her hand over his and took a deep breath. Her right foot found the edge of the boat, then her left. In a moment, she was on board, and Luke gave her a firm nod.

"Why Matilda?" Heather asked as she adjusted herself into a little seat near the staircase that went to the lower deck. Almost immediately, she regretted her question; she wasn't sure if she wanted to know all about Luke's previous love interests. She'd already dealt with simmering jealousy when it came to people like Monica from the records collection.

"Oh, gosh. It's a long story," Luke replied. He snapped the rope off of the dock and then cast them out from shore, hurriedly reaching to bring the sails out. They erupted, taking the air within them and then rushing into the waters beyond.

Heather forced herself to inhale, exhale. Bella and Kristine perched out of the way, captivated by the waters as they surged forward. Heather wanted to scream to the sky above. This was unnatural; the ocean was nothing but cruel.

"Was she the one who got away?" Bella called over the winds.

"Oh, no. Nothing like that," Luke told her as he steadied the sails.

"You're a mystery man, Luke," Kristine commented.

"I think it's good to keep some stuff to yourself," Luke told them. "Can't give away everything. Then where would your power be?"

"If Kristine tried to keep anything from me, I'd know about it," Bella said. "It's a twin thing."

"Ah. The famous twin thing. I wouldn't know anything about that," Luke offered playfully.

Again, Heather was faced with the dramatic truth: she knew nothing about this man. Nicole had said he was something of a wild card. But why? What had happened in his past? What was he running away from?

Bella poured champagne into little gleaming flutes. Heather gripped the stem with tentative fingers. She'd begun to count minutes, praying that they would make it back to land soon. It had been maybe ten minutes, maybe forever. Whatever happened, she couldn't let panic take over. Not then. It would distract Luke from his main task, which was ensuring her daughters were safe.

But Bella, Kristine, and Luke were fine. They cracked jokes, sipped champagne, spoke about the city. Luke had spent a bit of time there prior to his era in Bar Harbor. According to him, the city had changed a great deal since then. He described the bars and restaurants he'd once frequented, which, according to Kristine and Bella, had all closed in the past ten years. Luke grumbled inwardly.

"That's what I like about Bar Harbor. Things don't change that fast around here." He stretched his arms out toward the coastline. "People stick around. People care for what they have. Memories have greater density here because of it. For so many years, I didn't even understand the concept of solid ground. Now I do."

Kristine and Bella glanced at one another, seeming to have a conversation through the air. Heather very rarely understood what went on between them. It was that twin thing again.

She gripped the railing with white fingers, then forced herself to sip her champagne again. Years and years ago, Max had taken her out on a very similar boat. She'd had no fears. She had perched at the edge of the thing and dove into the waves, falling into the darkness and then erupting to the surface with laughter. Max had called her a wildcard, a free bird. She had even written a children's book about sailing— drawing the pictures herself that time, painting a portrait of her life with Max. One of eternal sunshine.

The waves crashed against the sides of the boat. Heather's nausea mounted. Max had been the strongest swimmer she'd ever known, the bravest man in the world. When the explosion happened on his ship off the coast, she'd envisioned a million ways he and the other crew might have survived. But days had turned to weeks, which had turned to months and still no body, no sign of life anywhere.

Why had she ever clung to any concept of hope? Was it just the way people survived? You needed something to hold onto. You needed land on which to stand.

Land— she needed to get to land. She needed her babies on land and stat. She forced her eyes to open and peered up at Luke, who was basically a stranger. His smile waned.

"Are you feeling okay, Heather?"

She cleared her throat. Bella and Kristine appeared on either side of him as though she was on trial.

"I can't. We have to— we have to go—"

She wasn't making sense. She closed her eyes again and felt on the verge of passing out. She dropped her flute of champagne, and the glass shattered from one side of the boat to the other. What a mess she was. Why had she come to Bar Harbor? Why had she thought her daughters could join her during this messy era of her life? She was no good for anyone.

Heather was in the midst of a full-fledged panic attack when Bella and Kristine insisted they return to shore as soon as possible. Luke asked if Heather was prone to these or seasickness. The girls replied no. That they should have known better than to agree to this, anyway. Heather felt utterly weak at this point.

Suddenly, there was the abrupt sound of the boat landing against the side of the dock. Heather's eyes opened enough to see Luke draw the rope around the dock and tie it tight. She rose and hustled off the boat as quickly as she could. Due to rushing, she fell to her knees on the dock and collapsed in a heap. Bella and Kristine called out. But just then, everything faded to impossible blackness.

There was nothing left.

AGAIN, there were voices around her. Heather felt far, far away, as though she floated in a dream.

"I should have brought us in sooner. She was looking pale even a few minutes in." This was Luke, who sounded inconsolable. "I wish she would have told me she didn't want to go. I would never have suggested it."

"She wanted to push herself." This was Bella.

"She's stubborn." Kristine was somewhere further away.

Heather still couldn't bring herself to open her eyes. Fatigue wrapped itself around her. Did she even have the muscles to stand? She wasn't on the dock anymore. Maybe somebody had moved her somewhere cozy. Maybe she was on her bed at home.

"You should tell the staff if you want anything— food, drinks, anything at all." This voice wasn't as familiar as the others. It was dark and raspy, yet somehow surprised.

"Thank you. And thank you for letting us use your couch," Bella said.

"When I saw you all on the dock, well..." The voice seemed hesitant to dive into any form of emotion. "I'm just glad we have this place near the docks."

"It means a lot," Kristine affirmed.

"Was it seasickness?" the voice asked.

For a moment, there was silence. Then, Bella said, "Our father died on the ocean last year. He was an oceanographer, and the boat had a gas leak which resulted in an explosion killing much of the crew. I don't think any of us have been on the water since."

"We should have known not to go," Kristine murmured as her voice bubbled with sorrow.

"That is an awful tragedy. I am terribly sorry for your loss." This was the voice again.

Something within Heather's stomach twitched with familiarity. Where had she heard this voice before? She had to wake up, had to see. She had to ensure her daughters knew she was all right. She'd made a mess of the day already. Maybe she could make an excuse. Say she'd eaten something bad for breakfast— anything.

Lifting her eyelids felt like lifting twenty-pound weights.

Clouds had shifted over Bar Harbor, thank goodness, and cast whatever room in which she now lay in an eerie, grey light. Bella sat in a chair alongside her. Heather herself was stretched out on a white couch in what looked to be a swanky beachside restaurant. As it was mid-afternoon, only a few guests lingered at various tables. Soft jazz music crept from the speakers.

"There she is," Bella breathed. She gripped Heather's hand harder, enough to remind Heather of just how alive she still was.

"Hi, honey." Heather's voice cracked.

Kristine rushed toward her with a glass of water. "Drink this. You're probably just dehydrated. Do you ever use that water bottle I got you for Christmas?"

Heather wanted to make a joke about Kristine being a mother hen instead of herself. But instead, she gripped the glass and sipped. Slowly, the world around her took on a more physical shape. Her eyes lifted over her daughters' heads to find Luke in conversation with a dark-haired, broad-shouldered man. Clearly, this was the owner of the deeper voice from earlier, the man who'd just learned about Max's terrible death.

The man alongside Luke was none other than Evan Snow, the very man who'd just kicked Luke and Heather out of his godforsaken mansion.

"What is he doing here?" she rasped then, just loud enough for Bella and Kristine to hear.

"Oh? He saw us on the dock," Bella explained. "He rushed out and helped Luke bring you in after you collapsed."

"But why him?" Heather demanded.

"He owns the restaurant, apparently," Kristine replied, glancing over her shoulder. "Do you know him?"

Heather closed her eyes again. All of this was a nightmare. Suddenly, the man who'd drawn a boundary between herself and her father's past had just learned about the single worst thing that had happened to her: Max's death. It felt too personal.

"Can we just head back home?" Heather whispered.

"Of course," Kristine said hurriedly. "I'll ask Luke if he can drive us now."

Heather spread herself out on the backseat of Luke's pickup, tucked safely behind Luke, Kristine, and Bella, who squabbled over which radio station to play before landing on a classic Queen song, which they sang in a beautiful chorus.

Before Heather had made her way out of Evan Snow's restaurant, he'd caught her eye and nodded to her, almost formidably. What had that nod meant? His eyes had told a far different story than before. It was as though he'd finally allowed himself to see her for who she really was. Heather wasn't entirely sure she liked that. It made her feel too vulnerable.

CHAPTER FIFTEEN

BELLA AND KRISTINE insisted that Heather take it easy over the remainder of their trip. Together, the three of them piled onto the living room couch, covered in old knitted blankets, pillows lush beneath them, and dove through old movies they'd watched years before— musicals and chick flicks and the occasional period drama, like *Pride and Prejudice*. At times, Heather pinched herself with disbelief. Her twenty-two-year-old daughters actually wanted to spend time with her, all the way out in the middle of nowhere, while the rest of the city raged on?

But there were definite sorrows within her daughters, reason enough for them to hide out with her. It went deeper than Kristine's recent breakup. Both girls had taken up therapists in recent months to deal with the death of their father. Only once, between chick flicks there on the couch, did they urge their mother to do the same.

"I don't know," Heather breathed. "I had that therapist for a few months immediately after the accident. I just felt like she did more harm than good."

"It's difficult to find a good therapist," Bella affirmed. She held a Twizzler aloft and moved it through the air as she made her point. "I tried out three before I actually went with this current one. Especially in the city, there are so many waiting lists—"

"Because everyone is messed up or crazy or sad or all three at once," Kristine interjected.

"Yes, exactly. But I'm glad to have found Evelyn," she continued. "She's a terrific person to talk to."

"Do you tell her stuff you don't tell me?" Kristine demanded then.

Bella wiggled her elbow into her sister's arm. "Don't be jealous of my therapist. I pay her to listen to me when you don't."

Heather giggled and snuggled tighter against her girls. Kristine suggested they watch Sweet Home Alabama next, a classic with Reese Witherspoon.

"Oh god, do you remember when Dad would imitate Reese when we watched this?" Bella asked as she hunted for the film.

"He killed that southern accent," Kristine affirmed.

Heather sucked in her cheeks with the memory. "That's right. He always said, 'You can take the girl out of the honky-tonk, but you can't take the honky-tonk out of the girl!'"

Kristine and Bella bellowed with laughter. Heather joined them, her eyes heavy with tears.

"And he said, 'Honey, just cuz I talk slow, doesn't mean I'm stupid,'" Bella added. "Gosh, for as much as he made fun of us for loving this movie, he really did have the whole thing memorized."

"That was your dad," Heather stated, feeling the nostalgia. "He was always willing to over-prepare when it came to making fun of us."

Heather rose and headed for the kitchen to grab a bottle of wine. Nicole then appeared on the other side of the glass, her smile bright, an attempt to hide her deep circles beneath her eyes.

"You're working yourself to death up there," Heather said somberly as she lifted the cork from the bottle.

Nicole shrugged. "It's a lot. And I know, sometimes I think I'm going a little crazy. But I take a lot of pleasure in it. It's been remarkable to see Bar Harbor open their arms to me as one of their own in hospitality. I walk into places sometimes, and I hear them say, 'There she is. The New Keating.'"

"The New Keating," Heather breathed. She placed four wine glasses in a row along the counter and clucked her tongue. "I wonder what Dad would have thought of you coming back and taking over his business."

This father who had left them. This father who'd been so terrifically depressed that he'd left the world of his own volition. This father she couldn't possibly understand. Who was he? Kristine and Bella had known their father; Nicole and Heather, and Casey had a far different story.

"I think about that sometimes," Nicole offered quietly. "Uncle Joe was terribly pleased, especially because his own daughter had never taken to the inn. He said the Keating Inn and Acadia Eatery had been his and our father's dream. That with every new pitfall and every piece of bad luck, they always knew they would always have this."

Heather's chin dropped toward her chest. "I wish we knew more about those pitfalls, about the dark times."

They held the silence for a moment. Nicole pressed a hand over Heather's shoulder and exhaled slowly.

"I'm guessing you haven't told the girls anything," she whispered.

Heather shook her head. "They're dealing with their own grief just now. I don't want to worry them with even more of my own."

"You're a good mother, you know."

Heather puffed out her cheeks. "Some days, I feel like the most incapable mother in the world."

The rain picked up outside as the wind howled against the windows panes like some kind of warning. Heather beckoned for Nicole to join the three of them in the living room to watch *Sweet Home Alabama*. Nicole ran upstairs for a moment to change into her pajamas, saying she couldn't bear to be uncomfortable while the others were so cozy.

While they waited, there was a dramatic knock on the door. The knock held nothing of the friendliness of Luke's knock. Heather placed her glass of wine on the counter and strode toward the front door. Bella and Kristine were in the midst of yet another argument about this season's boot style and whether or not it had all started with a Kardashian.

The disgruntled man on the other side of the door wore a dark raincoat, which shone from the intensity of the raindrops it now held. Beneath the hood, Heather made out a nearly familiar face. With a jolt, she recognized him as the butler of Evan Snow, Henry. In his hands, he held a large crate with what looked to be about three decades' worth of dust around the sides and underneath.

He held the box out in front of him for Heather to take. She did so, wrapping her arms beneath the dust. His eyes told her everything she needed to know: these were her father's things.

"Thank you..." Heather finally breathed.

"Mom? Is that the pizza?" Bella called from the living room.

Henry shrugged. "I just do as I'm told."

Henry then stepped back from the porch and disappeared again into the dark night. The box was so heavy that Heather's arms shook with fatigue.

"Mom?" Kristine called. "Do you need help?"

Heather hurried back into the foyer. "Not the pizza yet. Didn't they say another fifteen minutes?"

But already, Bella and Kristine had fallen back into their own conversation. This left Heather to sneak up the stairs to her bedroom and place the box on the floor. A brief inspection found several old-looking leather-bound books. And a slight peek into the front of one of them found the words: ADAM KEATING 1977.

1977. The year she had been born.

Her heart thudded as she stepped back. These diaries and documents were like ticking time bombs. They contained the truth. But was she ready to face it?

Before she returned downstairs, she grabbed her phone and, without thinking, dialed Luke's number. She had hardly spoken to him since the incident on the docks. Was it embarrassment that kept her away? Or just the intensity of her feelings for him? She didn't know. All she knew was that she needed him to know what had just happened. He was in this only because he wanted to be.

"Hey there. How are you feeling?" Luke's voice was warm and welcoming.

Heather's knees bent slightly. Would she fall to the floor all over again? "Hi."

"I've been texting you," Luke admitted. "And then I stopped texting you because I felt I was being annoying. But then, I was just thinking about texting you again."

Heather's lips curved upward. Downstairs, there was the doorbell and then the shuffle of her twins as they retrieved the two large pizzas from the delivery driver.

"Tell me, Heather. Are you all right?" Luke asked.

"I am. I really am." She swallowed the lump in her throat, then added, "I don't know what happened. I just lost my head."

"We've all lost our heads before," Luke said. "I just try not to do it when I'm out on the water."

"Yeah. Not great planning on my part," Heather affirmed.

Luke held the silence for a moment. Heather wanted to have him on the line as long as she could. After all the time they'd spent together, the past few days without him felt strange and off-kilter.

"I just received a special delivery from your old friend, Henry," she said finally.

"You're kidding."

"I know. He wasn't too happy to see me, either."

"Slimy little rat, isn't he?" Luke spat with a laugh. "What did he bring you?"

"A large box with diaries and some documents. That kind of thing."

Luke whistled. "Guess old Evan Snow got soft."

"You think he's taking pity on me?"

"There's no pity here. He had your father's things. And he saw you for who you really were the other day," Luke told her.

"Oh? Who I really am? A weak-willed woman apt to pass out at any given time?"

"No, Heather," Luke told her pointedly. "He saw you as a woman with a family. A woman people love. A woman who wants to know her story so desperately, even after so much heartache in the rest of her life. Evan Snow is a lot of things, but he's also a family man. And he had a tragedy of his own a few years back. His wife passed away."

Heather's heart dropped into her stomach. "That's awful. I wish I would have known."

"How could you know? Things happen to people. Bad things. And all we have to do is pick up the pieces and move on," he said.

She could sense that Luke spoke of himself here, too—whatever lurked beneath the surface, whatever darkness remained in his past. Still, this wasn't a phone conversation.

"I'd love your help if you're willing to give it," Heather asked then. "I know it's a big ask, but these diaries are terrifying for me."

"I'm there. You just say the word."

When Heather appeared downstairs, she found Bella, Kristine, and Nicole over the top of two large circles of cheese-laden crispy dough. Nicole lifted a glass of wine to her lips and giggled at something Bella said. It struck Heather as beautiful, seeing the three of them like this. Nicole hadn't spent much time with her girls since their big move to their universities, especially since Nicole had been in the midst of her own turmoil during those years. Probably, this was the first time Nicole really saw them as the women they'd become.

For the first time in ages, Heather considered Nicole's own relationship with her children, Abby and Nate. They'd never been particularly close. Heather realized, now, that Nicole hadn't mentioned them once. Heather's heart felt bruised. Could this have something to do with why Nicole had come to Bar Harbor in the first place?

Nicole commented on Bella and Kristine in the kitchen about halfway through *Sweet Home Alabama*, when she and Heather popped open another bottle of wine while Bella and Kristine ate their third slices of pizza— something Heather and Nicole resisted.

"They're such spectacular young women," Nicole complimented softly as she lifted the bottle of wine high over the glass. "I'm so grateful to get to know them in this new way. I remember going to your house last year after the accident— when we were waiting for news about Max, and I just looked at them and thought— well…" Nicole trailed off.

"They probably looked a lot like me," Heather offered. "Empty."

Nicole placed the bottle of wine back on the counter and wrapped her arms around Heather. Her chin nestled against her shoulder. "I'm so glad you three are here," she breathed finally. "Whatever happened in the past— between Dad or Mom or whoever else was involved— I'm glad that all that brought us together, here in this house, with the wild Maine rains outside the window. Can you imagine a better life than this?"

Heather's heart glowed with the beauty of it all, even in the face of such confusion. "I love you, sis," she whispered as their hug broke. "So glad my daughters have such a remarkable aunt like you. No matter what."

CHAPTER SIXTEEN

THE PASSAGE of time was a curse. All too soon, Sunday came, along with the first of two flights— one to take Bella and Kristine from Bar Harbor to Portland, and then another from Portland to New York City. Heather stood next to her Prius with her hand on her heart as she watched her gorgeous girls walk into the airport, one after another. Just when she thought they'd fully gone, they whipped open the door again and waved out. It reminded Heather of taking them to kindergarten some eighteen years ago when they hadn't been able to resist a final wave, a final hug. Just six or seven hours apart had felt like a century. Now, Heather wasn't sure when she'd see them again.

But there was so much to do, so much to discover. Heather draped her head against the back of the car seat as she eased back toward the main house, where Luke had said he would meet her that evening to pore over the documents and diaries. His text had read: "Maybe wine won't cut it tonight. How do you feel about whiskey?" To this, Heather had sent only a thumb's up. He got her. He got the heaviness of her situation.

Nicole had several appointments at the Keating Inn, which left the creaking, empty house to Heather and Heather alone before Luke's shift ended. She set herself up at the antique desk with the large, dusty box on her thighs. She'd turned on a stereo for background music, but it seemed too light-hearted to listen to pop music while she went through her father's old thoughts and feelings. If anything, her father was serious, literary— not the sort of man who would just listen to whatever was on. She got up and turned off the stereo, then lived in the deathly quiet.

Just as she'd suspected from the few leather-bound books she'd discovered so far, Adam Keating was a voracious writer and reader. Within this box, she found a number of old notebooks filled with poems and short stories. It was difficult to tell if these had been written prior to the ones she'd already discovered. It didn't matter, really. She simply relished the words. One poem, in particular, brought her to tears.

I wake in the morning to the sound of thunder
A young wife lies beside me—
And I know she could be any man's wife.
Why mine? What did I do to deserve such
Splendor.
Such is her beauty, her innocence as she
Sleeps on.
I marvel that it's up to me to calm the storm
For her. There's expectation in the "I do"
That I simply cannot meet.
When, pray tell, is love ever enough?

Heather had read countless autobiographies of other writers who'd only been discovered years after their death. Kafka, for example, had been a nobody for years and years; now, students pored over his texts at universities and discussed his prose at length. What would he have thought of all that attention?

She thought about bringing Adam Keating's words to the limelight. She was certainly a well-renowned writer in her own right. There was no reason she couldn't send some of his better things to her publisher.

Oh, but what good would that do anyone?

She continued to parse through the box. Eventually, she found another diary, written from around the same time as the previous one she'd discovered. For whatever reason, she still felt too frightened of the one from her birth year.

Within, she found that Adam wrote as a young father to a little baby named Casey. Apparently, these pages picked up where the last one had left off.

AUGUST 12, 1975

Jane glared at me all through dinner. She knows I'm boozing hard again. She smashed a plate in the sink and then, the baby began to wail. Poor little Casey, born to an absolute fool of a father and a beautiful mother who wanted nothing but to marry someone worthy. She didn't get that wish.

A few nights ago, she asked me what the hell I wanted from myself. I told her what I always tell her. That Joe and I have a plan. We want to open our own inn and restaurant. We want to cash in on real estate and the hospitality industry here in Bar Harbor. But more than that, we want to be a part of something major— something that matters. The way I see it, if you're a part of someone's vacation, you live forever in their memories. Maybe that's cheesy. Joe says it's romantic. I told him I'm nothing if not romantic.

Anyway, Jane, of course, brought up the realistic side of it all— that we don't have two pennies to rub together. I reminded her of the way we met. How we'd been so idealistic. How we'd told each other we'd be together despite everything. No matter how many stupid pennies we had jangling around in our pockets.

Heather flipped forward slightly in the diary. She sensed the sinister relationship between Jane and Adam, now. Had it all come down to money? As she and Max had always been generally comfortable, she couldn't fully visualize this strain, and she counted herself lucky because of it.

Still, she was mesmerized by his words.

OCTOBER 17, 1975

I don't know, now, if she ever truly saw me for who I was. I suppose that's typical for most romantic relationships. You draw up an idea of someone, and then they slowly begin to show you all the ways they aren't that person until eventually, you can't stand them anymore.

Is that where I am with Jane? I don't know.

I have a great deal of love for her even still— especially when I see her with Casey. Casey is such a happy baby girl. Always so bright, giggling, even sometimes in her sleep. Jane and I talk only of her if we talk at all. It's always, "Can you take her?" or "I already fed her," or "I don't suppose she needs a nap?" And it's never Jane and I asking one another if the other is okay. I supposed, when we married, that we were promising one another to care and care deeply all the days of our lives. I suppose marriage is a lie, just like all the rest.

Again, the concept of the elusive inn and restaurant came back up. Jane picked a fight about it, in fact. I suppose this was one time where she and I talked about something other than the baby. It didn't go well. She seems to eye the door. I want to tell her it's wide open for her.

But I can't. I love the baby too much. I don't want them to go. Plus, there's the issue of the new pregnancy. Due in April, I'm told. I have no affection for this new one. Why would I? The new baby was built from a loveless relationship. You can't build a full person from what we and Jane have together.

But what on earth would I tell Joe if Jane left me? That I failed at being a husband? That I have nothing to offer the world besides my own messes? What kind of person would get into business with a man like that, even if that man happened to be his brother? Joe is much smarter than that. No, he never had the grades I did; he's never read Proust or written an essay. But he's got a lot up there.

Heather's mind raced, now. Here she was, in the midst of the incredible horror of her father's life. Jane was pregnant with Nicole; Casey was a year and a half. Adam floundered, day after day, generally unsure where to turn or who to become. Jane had put the pressure on him.

Heather continued to sift through the pages. She was born in February 1977— which meant that her birth had been known midway through 1976. Around then, she found an entry that intrigued her.

. . .

JUNE 14, 1976

Darwin Snow has been gracious enough to hire me to manage a number of his properties. I already perceive Jane's affection for me rising. Still, I want to take issue with it. I want to demand of her— am I really better for her as a result of my income?

Still, it's not enough. With the new baby, we find new cracks in our already declining relationship. Casey is only two, but with that, apparently, comes a whole host of tantrums, many of which seem to be reflections of my inner soul and horror at the nature of our environment. I know, I want to tell her. I know we live in relative squalor.

Still, there was no mention of Heather's birth. She leaned back and flicked through the pages, then went on to the next diary— the one he'd listed as 1977. She flicked through this, until she passed all the way to February 25, 1977. Her birthday.

FEBRUARY 25, 1977

I barely made it to the hospital.

I had to sneak around, make excuses and find a babysitter for Nicole and Casey.

But it was worth it because I was there for her birth—a beautiful, beautiful baby girl.

Melanie gleamed with sweat and exhaustion. I held her hand and told her a story as she and the baby fell asleep. I told her, even so far into whatever consciousness she was, that we would find a perfect name for the baby.

Melanie is my soulmate; this new baby is my fresh start.

I can't believe I ever thought another world was possible.

This is it for me.

Heather jumped from her chair. Her entire body felt alert. She reread the diary entry from her birthday again as tears streaked across her cheeks.

Melanie? Who the hell was Melanie?

That moment, the doorbell rang. Heather placed the diary delicately on the desk, pressed her hands over her hair in a foolish attempt to calm it, then turned to march toward the foyer. When she opened the door, she found Luke, perfect, terribly handsome Luke, with his hand lifted to show off a large white doggy bag of the Eatery's best dinnertime food.

"I brought you dinner," he told her, still wearing that smile that seemed to pierce through time.

Heather's knees wobbled beneath her. In a moment, she felt she might crash to the ground. Luke rushed forward, gripped her elbow, and helped her walk to the couch.

"Heather? What's wrong? Heather? Gosh, you're white as a sheet."

Luke disappeared then reappeared with a glass of water. Heather drank it slowly. Her stomach, shrunk from her lack of eating, seemed to fill up from the water. She sputtered as Luke sat alongside her and reached for her hand.

"What's going on, Heather?" He finally asked it. He asked it as though it was one of the more difficult questions anyone had ever asked anyone.

Heather felt ridiculous. She sipped her water again and then said, "I think I know who my mother is."

Luke's eyes widened. "Tell me."

"I saw it in a diary entry from my birthdate. A woman named Melanie."

One of Heather's hands was limp, off to the left of the rest of her frame. Luke gripped it hard, a reminder that she remained on planet Earth.

"I have more digging to do. I just don't know how to do it alone."

Luke nodded. After a long pause, he said, "I think we're both starving after the past few hours we've had. How about we eat some food and drink some wine on the porch? Watch the sun set? After that, we can dive through your father's memories and figure the rest of it out."

Heather's nostrils flared. She gripped his hand harder. She tried yet again to remember what it had been like, a million years ago, to fall in love with Max. Had it felt anything like this? But no, it couldn't have. This was shadowed with so much trauma, probably on both sides. They were damaged people. Probably, Luke should run far, far away. Why hadn't he, yet?

"That sounds really lovely, Luke. Thank you."

"It's my pleasure," he returned. "Really."

CHAPTER SEVENTEEN

LUKE SET the table outside while Heather patched herself up in the bathroom. Her eyes were blotchy, red-tinged, and black streaks drew themselves from her eyes to her lips. Melanie— her mother's name was Melanie. The thought continued to ring through her skull. She eased a tube of lipstick over her lips and batted her eyelashes at herself, marveling at all the big decisions people made in their lives— decisions to cheat on their spouses, decisions to have babies, decisions to fall in and out of love. Life didn't just happen to you. Sometimes, you made it happen, too.

And what was she trying to make happen, with this lipstick, this dash of perfume? Did she have some sort of plot? She wasn't sure. Her mind raced with confusion. She heaved a sigh and then stepped into the hallway, where she padded downstairs toward the porch.

Luke had brought the Eatery's evening menu: a creamy shrimp pasta with garlic bread and a bottle of Domaine du Salvard

Cheverny Blanc 2018, which Luke introduced to her in a nearly-good French accent. Heather heard herself laugh, something she couldn't have imagined she might do again. Luke then pulled out the chair at the outdoor table and beckoned for her to sit.

"It looks delicious, Luke." She pressed her hands over her cheeks and begged herself, internally, to be normal. But what was normal, anyway?

Luke sat across from her after he poured the wine into glasses and lifted his toward her. "To Melanie," he said then. "Wherever she may be."

Heather's eyes were heavy with tears. She lifted her glass and clinked it with his. "It's just crazy to me that all these years, my family secrets have been latched away in some closet on the Snow property. My entire childhood with Jane and then with Aunt Tracy was all a lie. It's difficult to fathom."

Luke nodded somberly. He sipped his wine and then placed it on the table. Again, there was a heaviness to his face, darkness indicative of a long-ago era that Heather simply couldn't comprehend. And, due to this sudden eruption in life, as she knew it, Heather dared herself to ask.

"Why are you helping me, Luke?"

It was a simple enough question and one she'd already posed. It could have been perceived in many different ways. He pieced his fingers together beneath his chin and pondered the question for a moment. He seemed to weigh up the consequences of telling the truth. Always, when you told the truth, you paid for it in some way. Sometimes, the payment wasn't worth it. Heather knew this.

"I don't have the most perfect past, I suppose," Luke admitted tentatively.

Heather leaned back in her chair. Luke rolled pasta around his fork slowly, taking his eyes from hers.

"Bar Harbor isn't your home. You told me that," Heather murmured.

"Yes. But even the idea of home is a difficult one for me," he countered. He wore his crooked smile again, but this time, it was filled with sorrow. "I never really had one growing up."

Heather's lips parted. "What do you mean?"

Luke dropped his fork to the side of his plate. He sipped the wine again, seemingly trying to drop into some kind of haze in order to face his past. "The term orphan is such an awful term," he said then. "But I guess it applies to me in a nutshell. I was dropped off at an orphanage ten days after my birth. Ten days. I've thought endlessly about those first ten days. I guess I must have been with my parents during that time? They must have at least put in some kind of effort to keep an infant alive for ten days? But Jesus, how do you bring a tiny baby, your own baby, into an orphanage? What kind of horror happened to them that they couldn't bring themselves to..."

Luke trailed off. He dotted his napkin across his lips and shook his head, clearly frustrated. Heather pressed her hand across her heart.

"It must have been the hardest thing they ever did," she offered then, genuinely shocked. "Ten days with a baby and then..."

Luke shrugged. "I don't know. Maybe they were on drugs? Maybe they had no money? I can't even begin to fathom it. All I know is that there's no record of who they are. And then, around two years into my life at the orphanage, a wonderful thing happened. I was adopted."

Luke's face remained shadowed, proof that this seemingly "happy" occasion was anything but. "I stayed with the Humphreys for four years. Age two to age six. Formed some early memories there, I guess."

"Only four years?" Heather gaped at him. "What were they like?"

"It was almost like they were ghosts," Luke replied, his eyes swirled with an emotion she could quite put her finger on. "Never around and pretty negligent. They had a daughter who was older than me, and I remember her being the one to put together dinners for me and play with me in this little dirty room. You asked me about the name of my boat. Matilda. That was her name."

"Wow," Heather breathed, remembering how she'd thought the name had alluded to a previous love. How wrong she'd been.

Luke continued, "Eventually, someone called child services. It must have been someone at my kindergarten, although I'll never know for sure. Before I knew it, I was back at the orphanage—although it was the first time I really remembered it. Some of the workers there remembered me, though. They made me understand what a failure it was that I hadn't made it work outside the orphanage. And then, about a year after that came the Marvins."

Heather's fingers quivered with fear. She could already sense another horrendous story. And as Luke dove in, he explained that the Marvins already had seven kids, all of them older than him, most of whom made him pay for invading their already tight space.

"I got beat up for the first time there," Luke said with a sigh. "I had one toy, this little car a woman at the orphanage had given me, and one of the older kids decided that he wanted it instead. I fought tooth and nail for that car, but he was bigger, and he was meaner, and he wound up with the car and I ended up with a big black eye."

"Jesus," Heather whispered.

"I didn't stay at the Marvins longer than three years," he continued. "But by then, I was ten years old, and nobody was that interested in adopting an older kid, especially one with so many emotional problems. I ended up in a foster home later in Cincinnati. I ended up graduating from high school there and worked as many odd jobs as I could. Then I applied for scholarships so that I could get the hell out of Ohio. My god, I can't tell you how much I hate Ohio. Even seeing it on a map gives me the shakes."

Luke took a bite of his garlic shrimp pasta. Heather forced herself to follow suit. The flavor simmered with life; the texture was creamy and impeccable. Still, she'd never been less hungry in her life. After raising her two girls the way she had and living out her days as a children's writer, hearing about the horrors of the "system" in the United States bruised her soul.

"What happened to you is awful, Luke," she whispered. She stared down at her plate, still full of pasta. "You must think my predicament is nothing compared to all that."

Luke furrowed his brow. "That's ridiculous."

Heather stood on shaking legs and marched toward the edge of the porch. She gripped the railing and gazed out toward the haze of pinks and oranges and blues and yellows, a messy painted sunset. Luke joined her, just a few inches to her left. Far in the distance, a large boat blinked its bright lights as it steamed across the ocean's horizon.

"Everything I ever knew just flipped upside down," Heather whispered. "But that doesn't change the fact that I genuinely felt love as I grew up. My mother— the woman who raised me before her death was, in nearly every respect, Jane. My sisters, whether they're my half-sisters or not, were there for me in every way. They gave me love and support. They talked me down when I cried. They taught me how to ride a bike and how to do my makeup and how to deal with heartache. It sounds like your life in Ohio was just you against the world."

Luke gripped the railing with thick, powerful fingers. He looked on the edge of breaking down. She wondered how many people he'd explained this story to. Probably not many. "It felt like that. And when I left, I still felt like it was me against the world. It's meant that it's been difficult to really connect with people emotionally because many don't fully comprehend everything that's happened to me. How could they? But I've made myself an island of resentment. I don't know if that will ever really end."

Heather's hand flew over Luke's on the railing. His skin was rugged from the salty sea and the long hours in the kitchen.

"I want to help you find your family, the way you've helped me with all of this," she whispered then.

Luke's eyes widened. "I don't even know where to begin."

"It doesn't matter," Heather continued. "Since this all began for me, I've had you. I've had Nicole and Casey and even my daughters, bless them, who don't know anything that's gone on. All I've had are blessings. And I want to be that for you in some way if you'll let me. I know right now, more than ever, that you can feel lost without the truth. You must have felt lost all this time."

Luke's eyes shone. "I've felt lost every single day of my life."

It was impossible to know exactly how the next moments happened. When she asked herself later, Heather couldn't remember if she'd been the one to press forward or if he'd been the one to bridge the barrier between them. The only true thing was that suddenly, the two of them, both lost in the tumultuous seas of their lives, kissed there on the porch overlooking Frenchman Bay as the sun sank beneath the waters.

In the messy haze of the kiss, Heather closed her eyes and allowed herself to feel, really feel. But despite the beauty of it all, despite the aching of her heart, something in her stomach jumped with fear.

Max. She loved Max. How could she possibly love anyone but Max? It went against everything she'd ever known. She shivered and lifted her lips from Luke's. His eyes glowed with the orange from the sunset. He shifted his nose against hers. Her nose filled with his musk.

"I can't, Luke," she whispered as her voice cracked.

Luke pulled back the slightest bit so that their noses no longer touched. She suddenly felt sallow, weak. She removed her hand from his and stepped back toward the table. With a jolt, she recognized that she'd probably just added even more to the pain of his horribly painful life— another rejection.

But Luke was a grown man. He understood.

And if there was anyone in the world who could peer into Heather's eyes and feel the density of her soul, it was him. Somehow, it had always been him since her arrival to Bar Harbor.

"I feel so lucky that I met you, Luke," Heather said. "You've already changed my life."

Luke studied her. He crossed and uncrossed his arms over his chest. Finally, after a moment of horrible silence, he said, "You've changed mine, too."

He then stepped back. He slipped a hand through his hair and gestured toward his truck, which lurked just beyond. "I have to go."

Heather stuttered. "You've hardly eaten your dinner. Please. Stay."

But Luke scrambled for his things. "Don't worry about it. Pack it up. Make Nicole eat it when she gets home. God knows she hardly gets enough for herself, she's so busy up there." He then held up a hand before walking off toward the driveway.

Heather froze with fear and sorrow. The engine roared from the driveway. And in a moment, there was the creak of his tires as he rushed out of sight.

CHAPTER EIGHTEEN

HEATHER PACKED up the creamy pasta in Tupperware containers with the dutiful capabilities of a woman who'd once packed school and work lunches. The movements were so familiar to her; the muscle memory cast her down familiar lines of thought—thinking about Max out to sea, about her twins off in elementary school, learning to read. Every few seconds, she felt jolted back to the reality she now lived: here in Bar Harbor, miles from the home she'd once loved, on some sort of quest to uncover her true self.

And now? Now she had kissed her one true friend and probably ruined one of the more beautiful things she'd experienced in over a year.

Heather took the bottle of wine up to her bedroom, where she splayed herself across her pillows and blinked at the journals, which she'd piled up in front of her. They waited, expectant, all heavy with the story.

Heather flicked through the journal, back toward her birthdate, which she read again and again. According to Adam, Melanie was his fresh start. Melanie was his everything. And Baby Heather, who still didn't have her name, was a representation of that.

May 17, 1977

All this back and forth has made me wild with confusion. I feel tugged between worlds. My daughters— the three of them, are such shining beacons of light in my otherwise dark universe. My heart feels tugged between the three of them.

But Jane makes it nearly impossible to find solace in that horrible house. She demands so much of me. Although I've given my life to Darwin Snow, it's like it's never enough. She points to our negative bank balance and demands to know what sort of man I am. I tell her I love her, that I love our girls. She tells me I'm weak-minded.

By contrast, Melanie offers endless support. She knows I can't be with her and Heather, as often as I'd like to, knows that I have other responsibilities. I fall asleep in her arms, nearly crying, and she whispers that soon, we'll be together, that this will all be all right. I don't quite know how. She calms me, tells me that we'll get through this together. That soon, we'll be a family of three again.

A note about the name. About Heather.

When she was born, Melanie just put her own name on the birth certificate. She couldn't come up with anything— and I had to rush back to Casey and Nicole in the meantime.

But a week or two into Heather's little life, Melanie and I sat down together. We spoke in poetics about all the names we'd ever loved. Melanie had a thing for old actresses' names. Bridget Bardot and Marilyn Monroe. And little Heather, with that mole on her chin, seems to have this air about her— like she'll be someone someday.

Fame and fortune. I see it all for her stretched out like the stars in the sky.

I remembered a great-aunt I used to have a long time ago. She was the first person I ever knew who wanted more from her life than anyone else. She once gripped me on the shoulder and said, 'Adam, you can't allow the world to burden you. You're much stronger than all that. You see beauty where others see only darkness.'

I've never forgotten that.

Her name was Heather.

I explained this story to Melanie. Her eyes filled with tears. She sees the beauty in the darkness, too. She pressed her lips upon baby Heather's forehead and whispered, 'And so, her name will be Heather. Our angel, Heather.'

Heather squeezed her eyes shut. Was this true love between Adam and Melanie? Is this what you searched for— the kind of stuff you derailed your life for? She felt suddenly anxious and fearful, knowing that probably, she'd been the reason Jane and Adam had split up. But if she was the core of the love between Adam and Melanie, a love that seemed so pure and raw, then shouldn't she be grateful?

June 19, 1977

Jane packed up her things and took the girls and left today.

She told me she never wants to see me again— that the girls will have nothing to do with me— that I'm a sick and sorrowful creature she wishes she'd never laid eyes on.

The words felt like a damn curse. I hope somehow I can avoid whatever darkness she's thrown upon me.

Naturally, she learned of Melanie. Naturally, she learned of Heather.

Naturally, being Jane, she was smart enough to comprehend the weight of my love for another woman.

Minutes after Jane left, I rushed to the little seaside house where Melanie and Heather reside, dropped to my knees, and asked Melanie to marry me. Melanie flung her arms around my neck. I thought she might strangle me with happiness. I lifted her and spun her round and round while Baby Heather cooed in her crib, watching us. I know she'll grow up to feel a love I never fully knew as a young boy. Perhaps in this way, she'll never know the depression that constantly lurks behind my eyes. Maybe she'll only know sunshine and rainbows and wild afternoons of endless play.

A father can dream, can't he?

A father. Heather reread those words over and over again. Gratefulness permeated her soul. At least now, she knew: Casey and Nicole were surely her half-sisters. She could handle that.

But there were so many more questions at play. The diary was filled with another two years of entries. Her heart fluttered with apprehension. Couldn't she remain in this beautiful reality of these words from June 19, 1977? These words indicated a beautiful ecosystem for her, for Baby Heather. She'd known love between her parents. Maybe she had even emulated this love when she'd fallen for Max.

Bella texted her then. It was almost as though she sensed this major shift in the universe.

BELLA: Hey Mom! We finally got home just now.

BELLA: Remember, we're still very open to you moving to the city to pester us day-in and day-out.

BELLA: If there's anything writers love, it's city life, right?

Heather lifted her phone with shaking hands. She really did want to explain everything to her daughters; she just didn't know how right now. Hurriedly, she typed back:

HEATHER: Love you so much, Bell. Thanks for coming all the way here to see me.

She felt all the love her father had for her. It flowed through her, through this text message. Her heart pumped with it.

And at that moment, she had a strange memory— a memory of Jane bent over her bed and dotting a kiss on her forehead. "I love you so much," Jane had whispered. "Have sweet dreams, Heather-girl."

Jane. Why had Jane been her stand-in mother before her death?

What the hell had happened?

Her stomach quaked with anxiety. She poured herself another glass of wine and continued to read. Her eyesight grew blurry with each passing sip.

November 14, 1977

Melanie and I were married today in a small ceremony at the chapel by the sea.

The only people in attendance were my brother Joe and his wife, who held Baby Heather throughout.

Melanie glowed with beauty. She splayed her tender hands in mine and whispered that she would love me all the days of her life. My heart surged with love for her. I know we'll be happy— that no matter what comes for us, we'll find a way through the darkness together. It's the sort of love you read of in storybooks.

I can't believe I ever imagined similar ideas with Jane. I haven't heard from her at all since we finalized the divorce. I sometimes wonder about them— Nicole and Casey, who've begun their new life in Portland. They'll know nothing of my world here in Bar Harbor. They'll know nothing of their father, of what I love and what I dream of. They'll have only Jane's stoic face and Jane's practicality. Perhaps that's better in this cruel world. Perhaps I would have been better had I come out that way.

Heather flipped the page to another entry.

January 11, 1978

I knew everything would change for us.

Melanie gave me this impossible power. I spoke with Joe the past months, and we've orchestrated a plan— a plan to buy multiple properties across Bar Harbor and the rest of Mount Desert Island and create a Keating Empire. It sounds ridiculous, even to my own ears, but our funding has more than tripled in the previous few months, and I feel this incredible passion. I want to provide for my wife. I want to provide for my daughter.

Heather's heart thumped. If there was anything you could sense in this entry, it was a future collapse. Obviously, her father had committed suicide and obviously, he hadn't owned much more than the Keating Inn and Acadia Eatery in the wake of his death.

February 25, 1978

Heather is a year old today. I suppose Melanie decided that was a good enough day to pick another of her recent, ravenous fights with me. I've told her time and time again that I'm on the verge of something enormous. That rather soon, we might be rich, really rich. I've already purchased her some of the finest presents, gorgeous things that Jane would have leaped through the air to receive. But it somehow doesn't seem enough for Melanie, as though the more she receives, the less happy she is.

I know how women get after they tie the knot. Hell, Joe's

admitted that his wife can be this way, too. Needy. It's something in their evolution, I think. They need a protector. And I love Melanie and Heather to bits. I've put myself through the wringer to be that protector.

I told Melanie that our bank account is about ten times as stacked as it ever was with Jane, maybe even more. But she just ridiculed me for saying so. She spits at the mere idea of Jane— the woman who had two of my children.

Heather felt suddenly shattered from the words. How could her real mother be suddenly so cruel, even in the face of Adam making such changes?

And, according to the diary entries, the cruelty only mounted over the next year.

On her second birthday, in 1979, Melanie threw a pan at Adam's head.

February 25, 1979

I wound up in the hospital with blood pooling down my forehead, my cheek. Joe watched Heather back at home while Melanie cooled off at a bar downtown. I did something in that hospital room I haven't done in years. I prayed. I heard nothing from God above— wherever the hell he might be.

I wondered for the first time if I might have made a mistake.

I feel none of the love I once felt from Melanie. She's obstinate, ruthless and volatile, obviously. She heard a rumor that I'd flirted with a woman at one of the properties Joe and I now manage. It was a sincere lie, but she wouldn't hear it. She flung that pan and whacked me hard. I would never cheat on her; I've told her time and time again. At this, she cackles and says, 'Once a cheater, always a cheater.' I don't understand how that applies in this case.

After all, I only cheated on Jane once, and that one time resulted in all this. Our marriage. Our baby, Heather. Our enormous life together.

I feel just about as low as I ever have, and it's a funny thing, as right now, I have more wealth, more property, more on-paper accomplishments than I've ever had. I've thought about taking some of that money for therapy, but Melanie thinks therapy is weak. I suppose I agree, to an extent.

And I can't help but think if she'll just lighten all this pressure the slightest bit, if she only remembers how much love we once had, I could find a way back to the light again.

Heather paused before flipping to the next page.

July 15, 1979

There was no way I could have known.

No way I could have comprehended the weight of this evil.

But she's just served me with divorce papers from these swanky lawyers she apparently hired and pre-paid (all with the money I earned over the previous few years). Lawyers who've struck me with a whole list of demands. Lawyers who've arrived at some idea that despite the fact that Melanie hasn't done much over the years besides nag at me, she somehow deserves a whole lot of my property and wealth.

I don't even know if I have the energy to fight it.

Heather's hand formed a fist. How could Melanie do this, after everything Adam had done for her, for them?

September 17, 1979

A storm rages outside as I write this.

I sit in the Keating Inn's dilapidated restaurant, which Joe and I have lovingly called the Eatery. It's a hole in the wall—a place where you can buy soup and burgers, that kind of thing. Probably, within the year, that will be gone, too, just like everything else.

Melanie has already taken everything.

Funnily enough, she took the money and ran. She sold the properties back to the Snow family— who are back on top again as a result and shacked up with some guy near the mountains. His name is Jack. He's a carpenter. I want to wring his neck. I won't, though, because I'm not a monster.

That last note she left read: I'm not fit to be a wife or a mother.

And thusly, here beside me sits Heather. Poor, beautiful Heather, whose soul is just about as bright as the sun. She's my last link to a dying world. I wouldn't be here any longer if I didn't have to care for her.

Joe insists that Heather and I stay with him for a time until we get on our feet again. To hear him talk about Melanie is like listening to a preacher talk about the devil himself. Sometimes, it's funny to hear, but other times, it's like a constant reminder of what a fool I've been.

Jane. Casey. Nicole. The memory of them makes my heart ache with sorrow.

Heather stood as her mind reeled with all this information. She started pacing the floor while her thoughts ran rapid, and finally, her eyes fell on the diary again. She had to continue.

October 2, 1979

Drinking. It's been my near-constant release. Joe's wife takes Heather when I get too dark, and it allows me to spin further into chaos. I know I'm inches from some kind of death.

I went to Melanie's new place last night. I was drunk out of my mind, howling at her window from outside. Probably, if Jack had been home, he would have shot me through the stomach, but he wasn't.

I don't remember much from our exchange. I remember weeping and demanding how she could do this to me, to us? I remember asking her, 'Don't you remember how much love we had between us? Me, you, and our baby?'

And at this point, she scoffed and then she howled with laughter. She nearly fell to the ground with it. I thought she'd gone mad.

She wiped the tears from her eyes then, and she looked at me straight in the eye.

And she told me, 'You fool. Haven't you ever looked twice at that baby? That baby is so clearly not yours, you idiot. Heather was never yours. But you'll care for her. Because you're weak and you're soft and you would never turn her away now. Never.'

CHAPTER NINETEEN

HEATHER SNAPPED THE JOURNAL CLOSED. The words were like someone had punched her in the gut over and over again. She thought she would vomit right there where she sat. She stood and walked to the window, where she gazed out at the impossible darkness that lurked just beyond. The therapist she'd fired all those months ago had begged her not to dive into the depths of her thoughts regarding Max— had begged her to step away from her running ideas when she began to visualize Max's last minutes. Heather felt like a masochist. She was overly willing to assault her psyche. And now, she'd found another thing to throw into the mix.

Her mother hadn't wanted her. She'd used her as a sort of prop to ensure she could get close to Adam, build him up, and then steal his property and his money. She could imagine Adam: newly washed out of all his hard-earned money, with a weeping toddler on his knee. His love for Melanie and Heather had been powerful— a stone-built wall against any storm. He just hadn't imagined that the storm might come from within.

Downstairs, there was the click of the door. Nicole had returned. It was just after midnight, Nicole's usual arrival time. Heather was hungry to run down the stairs to meet her. But in these strange, somber moments, she felt outside of time and of family. The woman downstairs had no blood relation to her. Their relationship thus far had been a lie. Heather wasn't sure she wanted to face that just now.

Heather walked into the hallway and perched at the top of the stairs. Down below, Nicole fielded a call from one of her children. Her voice was calm, soothing as she spoke through whatever disaster Nate had gone through this week. Heather was vaguely certain that Nicole's daughter, Abby, wouldn't have called like that.

Heather remembered years before when Nicole's husband had abandoned them for a younger woman, and Nicole had had to rush into the safe haven of Casey's embrace. She'd resented that totally.

In the darkness of this hour, Heather got a sense of why Nicole had wanted to come all the way to Bar Harbor. Her marriage had faded. She hadn't had more than a few pennies to rub together. Uncle Joe's Keating Inn and Eatery beckoned, and she'd answered the call. Now, she'd flourished in a world she'd left when she'd been no more than a year old.

"Your Aunt Heather seems to be doing okay," Nicole said then. There was a soft knocking sound as she moved things around in the kitchen. Heather hoped she would find the food she'd set aside for her from Luke's attempt at dinner. What a failure that had been.

"Yes, she's still here. No, I don't think she's going to therapy anymore," Nicole continued. "I know. A tragedy like that..."

Heather shivered. She'd never heard one of her "sisters" discussing Max's death like this.

"I want to be there for her as much as I can. She and Casey would do the same for me. And they already did remember? When your dad..." Nicole coughed, then added, "I know. I promised that I wouldn't bring it up. I'm sorry. I love you, too. It's in the past. It's all in the past."

Heather felt the strange and sinister cracks of Nicole's past life, even from there.

Why hadn't Melanie felt this love for Heather? What had Heather been missing? What had she expected from motherhood, from marriage, that Heather and Adam hadn't been allowed? And who the hell was her father if Adam wasn't him?

Would the diary contain more answers?

Nicole continued the conversation with Nate.

"But gosh, I'm happy. Don't I sound happy? This place Uncle Joe and Dad left us, it's a dream. I can't wait for you to come to see it. We have to get the entire family together here. It's where it all started. It's what Uncle Joe wanted before he passed. I hate that you couldn't meet him. He had such a heart. During his funeral, everyone spoke about his generosity. How much he gave to this community. I just— well. Well, yes. To answer your question, it does make me so curious about my own father. I suppose I feel him here in some small way. I feel him in the water and the wind and the way they built up the restaurant. Uncle Joe said that me and Dad have a similar way of thinking, sometimes. It makes me a good hotel operator. Although, to be honest with you, honey, I have my eye on the Eatery. I know in my heart I'm meant to be a chef. I feel it."

Heather stepped back toward her bedroom, ducked back inside, and pressed the door closed. The way Nicole had spoken about Adam, about her father, felt like a funny punch in her gut. Uncle Joe had commented on their similarities. Probably, he wouldn't have said anything of the kind about Heather. Probably, he'd known all along what the truth of it all was.

Heather returned to the diaries. She couldn't help herself. She dug through the darkness now, hoping for some sort of reprieve, something that told her that no, in fact, Adam really was her father — that Melanie had said it all to be cruel.

October 15, 1979

I haven't gotten up from bed in many days.

I hear Joe down below with the baby. They've bonded over the previous days. Heather's giggling, a mad little happy toddler without any clue about the darkness of the world, and Joe is performing a little song for her, something to get the day started. He's asked me when I might feel up to coming back to work, to building back up the Keating Inn and Eatery in the wake of everything Melanie took. I know that when I look at him, my eyes reveal the dark holes in my soul. I have nothing for him.

November 22, 1979

Joe has begged me to do something else— anything else. I shot back nearly a fifth of whiskey and headed over to Melanie and her new boyfriend's to ask her the dreaded question: If I'm not Heather's father, then who is? But she slammed the door in my face and told me that it wasn't my business, nor anyone else's. I saw nothing of the bright and beautiful woman I fell in love with years before.

I've thought increasingly about Jane and the girls in Portland. Casey must be such a kid by now, probably drawing pictures and playing games. I imagine she'd just look at me like a stranger. No reason to remember who I am— that I fed and clothed and bathed her and that I sang her to sleep. In the end, the only thing that matters is that I, ultimately, abandoned her and Nicole and their mother. I suppose I'll never forgive myself for that.

It is my cross to bear if I am even brave enough to bear it.

Of course, suicide crosses my mind.

Heather's stomach seized. She erupted from bed and rushed toward the bathroom. She imagined she might vomit but only hovered over the toilet, waiting. After five or ten minutes, she returned to the bed and flopped back.

November 23, 1979

It's Thanksgiving Day if you can believe it. Little Heather sits in her high chair and smashes a plastic spoon across the little table as Uncle Joe and his daughter, Brittany, stir up stuffing and cranberries. Brittany has really taken to little Heather. A darkness within me wants to tell Brittany that no, Heather isn't her cousin; she's not related to any of us. But how can you say such a thing about such a creature, with such bright sapphire eyes? I still love her. I've spent her whole life loving her. It won't just go away like that.

It occurred to me, though, that I can't trust myself to care for her. Joe is weighed down with Brittany and his own wife, and we want to press forward on the Keating Inn and Eatery. It's a rare thing for me to have enough energy to get through the day, let alone ensure Heather is fed.

I think of Jane. Of how good she was. How pure. How she looked after Casey and Nicole despite whatever inner chaos she dealt with. Sometimes, we would have these insane blow-outs— fights that lasted the whole night and she would go sing to the girls to wake them up, as though her night's dream had been nothing but rainbows.

I can't imagine a better mother for this poor, sweet child.

But why on earth would Jane say yes? When I posed the idea to Joe, he scoffed at it. He demanded why I should put more pressure on Jane. I told him that my life, as I currently know it, is in life-or-death mode. That shut him up.

I'll send her a letter. I'll explain as much as I can. Jane will do what she'll do.

Happy Thanksgiving to me, the poor sap who fell in love and subsequently lost his mind and his fortune. I still have so much for having so little. And I'm sure I'll even squander that along the way.

Heather's eyes filled with tears. She pressed the book against her chest and gazed out the dark window. The clock read just past four in the morning. How was that possible? She knew in her soul she wouldn't sleep, not that night and maybe not ever again. She again shifted toward the wardrobe and opened the drawer to spot Max's package of cigarettes. She felt akin to Adam, miles away from anything she'd ever known, and not entirely sure anything would be all right again.

Time changed after that. It seemed to shift and morph as Heather sat in the silence of her bedroom. When eight o'clock shone brightly on the clock, Heather felt as though only two hours had passed. She lifted herself from bed and stretched her arms over her head. Her bones creaked. It seemed incredible that she still had a body when the world had shifted so much.

Downstairs, she found Nicole at the table, listless, staring into a bowl of cereal. She grumbled, "Good morning," then took another bite. It looked like Shredded Wheat. Heather couldn't imagine ever being hungry again.

Nicole's eyes found Heather's. Heather demanded herself to sit down, to pour herself a bowl of cereal, to concentrate on something other than the diaries. She found herself with her spoon poised through the milk, just as Nicole's phone blared.

"Hello, this is Nicole Harvey speaking."

A little wrinkle formed between her brows. She placed her hand over her mouth. After another pause, she said, "Yes. We'll be there right away."

The DNA test results. Heather knew, with a funny jump in her stomach, that that's what the call was about. Nicole grimaced. She lifted her eyes toward the woman who'd once been her younger sister and said, "Do you want to go pick them up together?"

Heather felt armored against the truth. She latched herself in the front seat of Nicole's car and remained silent as Nicole eased them toward the test center. When Nicole sat alongside her with the test results in her hand, she said, "You know, whatever's in this envelope doesn't change anything. We still have our memories. We still have our love. We're still sisters, always." Her eyes brimmed with tears.

But Heather already knew what the results would say. Nicole slipped the piece of paper from the envelope, read the results to herself, then pressed her hand over her mouth.

After a long, horrible pause, Heather whispered, "I'm not related to you or Casey or Mom or Dad, am I?"

Nicole's eyelids dropped over her eyes. A tear fell down her cheek.

"Does it say who my parents are?"

Nicole cleared her throat. "DNA analysis says their names are Roger Conrad and Melanie Hyde."

"Roger." The name felt so foreign across her tongue.

Above, the rain had begun again. It splattered across the window pane. She shivered, then cast herself into the side of the car, gripping the handle to put her foot on the pavement.

"Where are you going?" Nicole cried.

But Heather couldn't remain in that car. She couldn't sit still. She rushed into the grey morning rain as her clothing became drenched all the way through. She wished she could stop feeling the way she did. She wished she could remember what it felt like to belong.

But just then, she felt utterly alone. And she had a hunch she knew who else felt like that, too.

CHAPTER TWENTY

HEATHER PUSHED her hands in her pockets and hovered at the edge of the sidewalk, waiting for the light to change. She had very little concept of time. When the green light flashed for pedestrians, she staggered across and then hustled up the staircase that led to Luke's house, a mere fifty feet from the edge of Frenchman's Bay. She'd always known where his little place sat but had never actually been inside.

On his doorstep, Heather shifted beneath the overhang to ensure rain couldn't catch her. She turned her eyes toward the boats, latched along the docks nearby. They clicked against the wood of the docks, kicking themselves to and fro with the waves. Far above the little town, Cadillac Mountain surged into the fog. For not the first time, Heather was captivated by the beauty of this place. She wished she could see it with her father's eyes. Probably, after everything Melanie put him through, he'd been unable to experience the glorious view. His world had turned dark even before he'd decided, once and for all, to turn off the lights.

The door opened even before Heather could knock. She lifted her eyes to find Luke's. Beneath his bright green irises, dark shadows crept in half-moons. Maybe he hadn't slept, either.

"Heather," he whispered. His lips seemed to cradle her name as though it was the most precious thing to him in the world.

Heather's knees clacked together. Hurriedly, Luke placed a hand on her shoulder and led her inside, where he insisted she remove her wet clothing. He rushed into a back room and then returned with a large sweatshirt and a pair of flannel pants. While Heather waited, dripping, she assessed the space around her. It was a comfortable house. Perfect for a bachelor, with a cozy armchair and couch that was a soft blue-green color. In one corner was a moderately-sized television and a brick fireplace, in which a fire sparkled Toward the left, there was a small kitchen with an island, on which now sat a steaming pot of coffee and what looked like freshly baked banana bread.

"Will these do?" Luke lifted the clothes toward her.

"Gosh, yes. Thank you." Heather was surprised that her voice had any power at all.

Luke turned and headed back toward the kitchen. "The bathroom is just off to your right."

Heather stepped inside, clicked the door closed, and removed her drenched clothing, one piece after another. She used a clean, folded-up towel from the rack and dotted her face, her hair, then slipped into the soft sweatshirt and flannel pants, which she rolled up to her ankles, as they were much too tall for her.

The mirror told her a sorrowful story about her face. She sorely needed some foundation and eyeliner and mascara. But, she supposed, after all she and Luke had been through— both together and apart— she could afford looking like a crypt-keeper. At least for a little while.

Luke placed two small blue plates on the counter, on which he slid slices of banana bread. He poured her a steaming cup of coffee, then gestured toward the little sunroom toward the back. It glowed with soft morning light, protected from the rain, and offered a gorgeous view of Frenchman Bay. Heather's heart skipped a beat.

"Don't you have a beautiful, safe haven here," she whispered as she carried her bread and coffee to the cozy sunroom.

She sat across from him on a little dark red cushion. He placed his uneaten banana bread on the table between them.

"I'm sorry for last night," he finally said. "It's a really rare thing for me to tell anyone my past. It probably made me feel closer to you than I should have allowed myself to feel."

Heather's heart cracked at the edges. She reached out and splayed her hand over his, there on his knee. Their eyes locked. She really could have kissed him again. She could have grown addicted to that rushing feeling, as though gravity itself no longer existed.

"I feel really close to you, too," she whispered. "I just don't know what to do about it."

"I never know what to do," Luke told her with a little smile.

"Then where does all that confidence come from?"

Luke's laugh was deep, troubled. "I've just been making it up as I go along all these years."

Heather sipped her coffee. The warm, nutty flavor descended over her tongue. Again, her phone buzzed with a call from Nicole. She just couldn't face her. Not yet.

"You know something else, don't you?" Luke finally asked.

"How can you tell?"

Luke lifted his shoulder the slightest bit. "Growing up the way I did, I had to learn how to read people. If they were angry, I had to learn to get out of their way."

Heather's eyes welled with tears. Luke gripped her hand.

"You're not alone in this," he reminded her.

"Not like you were," Heather agreed. "I know that."

"My trauma and pain are immeasurable, but it's not the kind of thing you can compare," Luke told her. "All we can do for one another is hold each other up. Even if you can't—" He trailed off as his eyes dropped.

Heather had to assume he wanted to say, *'Even if you can't love me.'*

But maybe she could. Maybe she really could.

"Adam's diaries told a horrible story," she admitted finally. "My mother manipulated him into falling in love with her and believing I was his daughter. She blew the wind into his sails, only to rob him of his fortune and leave him with a toddler who, ultimately, wasn't his own. With his past history of depression, he didn't stand a chance. He couldn't raise me, and he couldn't find it within himself to ask his brother, Joe, for help."

"So he turned to his ex-wife," Luke guessed. He leaned back as he puffed his cheeks full of air.

Heather nodded. Her eyelashes dropped over her cheeks. Again, the subtle dab-dab of the rain across the glass was soothing against the panicked waves of her brain.

"Have you told Nicole?" Luke asked.

"She sort of knows. We received the DNA results just now, and

I just— I couldn't even look at her," Heather whispered. "We've all carried this lie together, without even knowing about it."

They held the silence for a moment. In the distance, near the docks, a dog howled out toward the boat, far off along the horizon, as though he had something really important to say. Max had always wanted a dog. Why hadn't they gotten one? Heather half-remembered telling him she didn't want to clean up dog hair half the day. He'd teased her that her own hair, which was dense and often shed, was enough clean-up for the both of them.

"Why didn't you ever want a family of your own, Luke?" Heather asked then, surprising herself.

Luke's cheek twitched.

After a pause, Heather breathed, "I'm sorry. That was way over the line."

"No, it wasn't. I'm just trying to figure out how to answer."

Luke sipped his coffee and then pressed on. "Being tossed around like that throughout my youth made me feel like poison. I noticed a shift in the dynamic in every new home I entered. The other kids looked at me like I'd destroyed something very special. I could never know how things had been prior to my arrival. Probably, things had been just as bad, but with me there, they had a new scapegoat.

"I guess I had myself convinced, at some point, that I couldn't bring children into this world. That I would poison them the way I'd poisoned everything else. Women came and went. Some of them asked me to go in that direction with them. I refused." Luke's eyes were tinged red with sorrow. "I missed my chance, I guess. It's incredible to me that one day, you can just wake up and realize the boat's left without you. But that's how time goes."

Heather's heart pounded louder and louder. She squeezed Luke's hand. "Bar Harbor residents love you, Luke. They don't see any poison in you. I see it in the way they look at you. The people at that little bar think of you like their pride and joy. My sister thinks you're a piece of work, but in the best way."

Luke chuckled lightly, even as his eyes glowed with tears. "I know what I have here. I'm so grateful for it, really. I wake up every morning and thank God above that I'm not ten years old and terrified out of my mind at one foster home or another. I have this safe place. I have an incredible job. And now— well, I have a really wonderful, perhaps overly beautiful friend. If only you weren't so damn beautiful."

Heather closed her eyes as a laugh bubbled up from her stomach. Luke joined her. Maybe they would forever live in the in-between of their attraction. Maybe their friendship would always hinge on this joke.

When she opened her eyes again, Luke nodded and said, "So. What's the plan today, then?"

Heather arched her eyebrow. "What do you mean?"

"Do you want to find your mother, or what?"

CHAPTER TWENTY-ONE

MONICA from the records office nearly screeched with pleasure when Luke marched up to her desk. She jumped up and spread her manicured fingers across the counter. Her eyes hardly registered Heather directly beside him as she took in full view of this rugged, handsome man.

"There you are," she purred. "I haven't seen you at the bar this week. Worried we scared you away."

"Been busy, is all," Luke replied. "Life as a sous chef isn't the easiest."

"You'll be the big boss one day," Monica told him.

"And so will you," Luke told her. "Someday, you'll rule this town from the record office all the way to the top."

Monica blushed and swept a blonde curl behind her ear. She then turned her eyes toward Heather and gave her a little up-down as she assessed Heather in Luke's sweats. "What can I do for you two today?"

Back in the record collection, Heather gave Luke a cheeky grin and said, "You know how to get what you want, no matter what, don't you?"

Luke shook his head. "No way. And before you ask me if I feel guilty about old Monica over there, I'll tell you for sure she has about three boyfriends right now, all of whom are head-over-heels in love with her— as they should be. She's certainly not my type at all."

He fluttered his fingers over the birth files in February of 1977, the same files they'd parsed through weeks before. Here, he drew out a file that read Melanie Hyde— the birth certificate for Heather, from all those years before, when Melanie and Adam hadn't yet arrived at the name "Heather" and had put a filler of Melanie's name. Below, beside Father, Adam Keating's name was listed; below that, Melanie Hyde was listed as the mother. They'd both given their signature— two foreign-looking swooshes in faded blue ink.

"She had him fooled from day one," Heather whispered in disbelief. "My birth unraveled his entire world with Jane, Nicole, and Casey. Like a bomb went off."

It was difficult for Heather to comprehend what might happen if and when she encountered Melanie. On the drive over to the record office, she'd half-imagined herself finding Melanie still up in the mountains with the man she'd left Adam for. She'd be in her sixties, probably— maybe a direct reflection of Heather herself, who'd always struggled, now that she thought of it, to see herself in her sisters and her stand-in mother, Jane.

Her mind had often given her the term "sociopath" while she'd read over the diary entries. What kind of woman could have done what Melanie had done? What had brought her to such cruelty?

And worst of all, did Heather have any of that cruelty within her?

What was it her other mother, Jane, had always said to Casey, Nicole, and Heather?? "Kindness. It costs nothing but means everything." Aunt Tracy had said the words in the years after Jane's death, taking up the narrative. Kindness seemed a foreign concept to the likes of Melanie Hyde.

"So I guess we're searching for a record of Melanie Hyde," Luke said. He splayed the birth certificate out on the counter between them and then returned to the front desk to retrieve Monica.

Monica returned, typed the password into the computer to enter, and then instructed them on searching through current records, which had been moved online five years before.

"It took us some time to move into the twenty-first century," she told them pointedly. "But now that we're here, it makes everything a whole lot easier. Are you looking for lost family members? Lots of people are hungry for their family tree, now that Ancestry dot com and Twenty-Three and Me are so popular. Here, just type who you're looking for here..." She gestured toward a little empty box and then headed back up to the front desk, where someone waited for her.

Heather poised her fingers over the keyboard. With tentative motions, she typed out, "Melanie Hyde," then let it sit there for a moment.

"Some part of me doesn't want to know," she admitted to Luke. "This woman was cruel and manipulative. She left me with a man who wasn't my father after she stole everything from him. She led Adam to kill himself, and I'm pretty damn sure she didn't care."

Luke nodded. "But I still understand this desire to know. I've had it all my life."

Heather clicked enter.

Almost immediately, the screen flung up a single result:

MELANIE HYDE

BIRTH: March 17, 1954, Bar Harbor, Maine

DEATH: October 7, 1999, Bar Harbor, Maine

Heather fell back into the chair just behind her. She gaped at the word: DEATH. In the span of a single day, she'd learned of the existence of this other mother. She'd lived. She'd given birth. She'd done a hundred cruel things and perhaps some good things, too, and then had died at the age of forty-five. She'd lived only one year beyond Heather's current age.

"Jesus," Heather whispered.

Luke spread a hand over her back, an offer of comfort. Heather was listless.

"She's gone," Heather said finally.

"What about your father?"

Heather investigated Roger Conrad and found that he, too, had died. Her heart dropped into her stomach.

"I'm an orphan in so many different ways," she lamented, her voice breaking.

According to the server, Roger Conrad didn't have any family leftover in Bar Harbor or surrounding areas. Melanie, however, did.

"Kim Hyde Robinson." Heather breathed the name to herself. "Her sister. She had a sister."

She was listed as a divorced mother of two, born in Bar Harbor two years before her sister, Melanie. This made her sixty-nine years old.

"There's an address," Luke pointed out.

"Yes. I see that." Heather felt as though she walked on hot coals.

"You want to go check it out?" Luke asked.

HEATHER TYPED Kim's address into her phone's GPS and watched as the rain pattered across Luke's truck windows. Luke was quiet, capable at the wheel, knowing full-well that conversation wasn't in the cards for Heather, not now as her mind raced.

Again, Nicole texted her.

NICOLE: I'm super worried about you.

NICOLE: I'm at the inn.

NICOLE: Come find me when you feel up to it.

NICOLE: I don't like feeling like you're out there on your own, dealing with this.

NICOLE: I want to help you carry it.

NICOLE: Please.

Heather pressed her lips together, reading and re-reading the messages. When Luke hovered at a stop sign, she typed.

HEATHER: Please, don't worry about me. I love you.

It had to be enough for now.

As they passed the Keating Inn, however, Heather snapped her fingers and said, "I can't meet my aunt in your clothes, Luke."

Luke gave her a sneaky grin. "What do you have against my fashion-forward sweats?"

"Absolutely nothing if I planned to eat ice cream all day," Heather said. "If you could just stop by the house..."

Luke nodded. "Already ahead of you."

Heather hurried into the house, which was blissfully void of any prying eyes from Nicole, headed upstairs, changed into a black dress and a pair of tights, grabbed her raincoat, then, after a pause, placed the relevant diaries into her purse, just in case Kim needed proof. She added just a dash of makeup but left her hair in a heap of curls due to the rain. She looked half-frantic but beautiful, like a character in a dramatic eighties movie. It would have to do.

And when she hopped into Luke's truck a few minutes later, he whistled and said, "You were gone ten minutes, tops."

"Impressed?"

"You're a different kind of woman, Heather Harvey," he teased. "I'll give you that."

Kim Hyde Robinson's small yellow house was located about a half-mile from the shoreline, where the land began to curl toward the Acadia Mountains. Her house was shrouded with gorgeous, full trees, the leaves of which pooled down to capture the thick raindrops from above. Luke ballooned an umbrella over them both and hustled Heather up to the doorstep. Once there, Heather marveled that this was the second time she'd just appeared at someone's door like this— first Evan Snow, now this.

In her past life, she would have never done something like this. She would have told Bella and Kristine that it was an invasion of privacy. That it was polite to call first.

Still, as she lifted her fist to the door, she was reminded of the bravery of some of the children in her books. They'd had to find impossible strength within themselves to press forward, to learn and grow. Even at forty-four, she had to find it within herself, as well.

Heather knocked twice before she heard a fluttering of feet behind the door. Nervous, she assessed the garden decorations and the birdbath off to the right. Everything looked clean and bright, well-taken-care-of. Had Melanie ever been to this house before? Had Melanie ever planted a garden? Had Melanie—

Before Heather could continue her panicked thoughts, a woman opened the door and blinked out.

Heather felt punched through the stomach almost immediately at the sight of the woman's eyes. They were bright sapphire, enormous, just like Heather's. Although it was probably a dye job, the woman also had jet-black hair, just like Heather. Even her nose was shaped similarly, with the slightest hook at the end.

The woman peered at Heather curiously, as though they'd met before, yet she couldn't place her.

"Can I help you?"

Heather's throat tightened. She gripped the umbrella's handle so hard, she thought the wood might crack.

"I'm really sorry to barge in on you like this," she said, sounding clumsy. "It's just that I— well, I have a very sensitive issue to discuss with you. It's a family matter."

The woman furrowed her brow. "Is this about one of my kids?"

Heather shook her head. "No. It's about your sister. It's about Melanie."

Kim's lips parted. She beckoned for Heather and Luke to step inside, out of the rain. Once there, Heather placed the folded-up umbrella on the coat stand and removed her coat, grateful she'd taken the time to don something more presentable. Although Kim had obviously planned to spend the day indoors, she'd still put on a pair of jeans and a black turtleneck, both of which highlighted her still-powerful, lean figure.

She was sincerely beautiful.

"May I offer you two some tea?" Kim still looked terribly confused.

Before Heather could answer, Kim turned on a heel and led them into the small living room with its attached kitchen. There, she placed a kettle on the stove. Behind her, the clock read 11:13. Heather had lost all concept of time.

Kim sat on the easy chair and beckoned for them to sit across from her on the couch. The water remained silent on the stove for the time being. Kim's sapphire eyes tried to dig into Heather's similarly sapphire ones.

"You said this was about Melanie." Kim finally broke the silence.

"Yes." How could she possibly name everything? "I'm terribly sorry for your loss."

Kim nodded firmly. "Thank you. Well. To be honest with you, prior to her death, Melanie and I hadn't spoken in decades."

"Decades?" Heather couldn't imagine going a month without speaking to Nicole or Casey in some way, let alone decades.

The water began to roar from the stove. Kim hopped up and poured the tea, seemingly grateful to have something to do with her hands. "She was a piece of work, my sister. Always after everyone else's money. She borrowed from my husband and I endlessly and never paid us back. That's not why we parted ways, though. She took our mother's locket without asking. Sold it and took all the money. Around that time, my husband landed a job in Bangor, and I got pregnant with my daughter. I wanted nothing to do with Melanie or with Bar Harbor at the time. By the time my children and I returned to Bar Harbor, in fact, Melanie was already dead."

Heather's heart cracked at the story. She dropped her shoulders as Kim placed the two cups of tea before them. Luke took her hand.

"I've just learned that Melanie was my mother," Heather said finally, pressing through the silence. "I have a photo of the birth certificate to prove it."

Kim's face echoed her profound shock. She gaped at the photo Heather had taken at the record office, then fell back on the couch, nearly spilling her tea.

"You're such a Hyde girl," she whispered in disbelief. "I knew it when I opened the door. But her daughter? Melanie's daughter? How did I not know?"

Heather knew she would have to explain everything. It would take time. It would be painful. But Kim's eyes were hungry for the story. She took a small sip of the piping hot tea, then dove in—describing where she'd grown up and everything she'd learned in the previous few weeks. The story took well over an hour, during which none of them took a sip of tea, which they allowed to cool to room temperature, forgotten.

With the story complete, Kim placed her cup of tea off to the side, rose, and closed the space between them. Heather fell forward into her embrace as tears rolled from her eyes. Even the way Kim smelled seemed familiar, like a piece of a puzzle she'd long-ago lost.

When Kim dropped back, there was the sound of the front door opening. Almost immediately, there was a scrambling sound of soft feet, then the call of an adult. "Mom? Mom, are you home?"

Heather's heart surged with fear. She glanced leftward toward Luke, whose lips were parted with disbelief. Her family was here. They'd been all around her, all this time.

CHAPTER TWENTY-TWO

THE WOMAN who appeared around the corner had jet-black hair and, yet again, those bright, sapphire eyes. In front of her, a toddler wobbled around on bright red rain boots; two ocean eyes peered out from beneath a mop of black hair. He grinned at Heather and then placed his teeth nervously over his lips. The woman above gave her a bright, confused smile, then said, "Hi there. I'm Jennifer." She then gave her mother a curious look, dropped down, and lifted the toddler against her. "Mom, I picked up your prescription on the way."

"Thank you, honey." Kim seemed unsure of how to proceed.

Jennifer stepped through the living room and headed for the kitchen, where she removed the prescription bag from her purse and placed it tenderly in a little wooden bowl. Her actions seemed so second-nature, so easy, as though she'd performed them time and time again for centuries.

How strange to have a mother to care for. How strange to live out this cozy existence alongside your loved ones without the horrible secrets echoing from your past.

"Jen, this is Heather and her friend, Luke," Kim said finally. She stood and walked, like a sleepwalker, into the kitchen. "Heather and Luke, this is my daughter, Jennifer, and her grandson, Oliver."

Jennifer gave Heather another pained smile, then turned to face her mother. Under her breath, she muttered, "They aren't here selling you anything you don't need, are they?"

Kim shook her head as color returned to her cheeks. "You know I'm not a dummy, Jen."

Jennifer adjusted Oliver against her hip. "I know that, Mom. You just have to be careful about scammers."

Heather's heart thudded with apprehension. This woman that looked to be close to her age was her cousin. Perhaps, in another reality, she and Jennifer might have played together on the shoreline. Perhaps, their children would have been friends with one another. Perhaps they would have been a part of the vibrant community of Bar Harbor— sailing and picnicking and hiking through the mountains.

Kim's eyes filled with tears. She'd hardly kept it together through the story. Now, Jennifer stepped back, shocked. Oliver wiggled out of her arms and then rushed toward Heather, where he placed his little hands on her knees and gazed up at her.

"Is he two?" Heather asked.

"Nearly," Jennifer offered. "My daughter had him at nineteen if you can believe it. It shocked us to our core. But now, we can't imagine life without him."

"Of course," Heather replied. She made a little face at Oliver as Jennifer returned to Kim and muttered, "What's going on?"

"I forgot to ask," Kim finally said, her voice directing toward Heather. "Do you have children?"

"I do," Heather said brightly. The memory of their beautiful faces lifted her. "Kristine and Bella. They're twins. Twenty-two years old. They both live in New York City."

"The city, wow," Jennifer said with a sigh. "I lived there briefly, oh, twenty-four years ago."

"The most anxious time of my life," Kim affirmed with a laugh. She lifted a Kleenex, then dabbed it over her cheek. Finally, with another horrible sigh, she said, "Jennifer, you never met your Aunt Melanie. Apparently, Melanie had a daughter. And Heather is that daughter."

Jennifer's mouth flew open. Oliver smashed his palm against Heather's knee again with glee, as though he'd felt the drama in the room and decided to take it upon himself to boost it.

Heather shook her head and tried out a smile for the first time. "It's really, really new to me, too."

"Oh, you poor thing," Jennifer said. Hurriedly, she reached into her purse and drew out a large brown bag. In a flash, she poured a selection of fluffy-looking croissants into a clean bowl and placed it at the center of the table. "I don't know what else to do but feed you."

Heather laughed. "That's my instinct, as a mother, too."

Kim and Jennifer sat across from Luke and Heather. Oliver crawled into Jennifer's lap as she shook her head in disbelief.

"She left you," Jennifer repeated softly, after a bit of the story had been repeated for her ears. "That is so awful."

"She was a selfish woman," Kim remarked. "Sometimes, she could be selfish as a little girl, too. Volatile. All over the place, emotionally. My mother never knew what to do with her."

"And the woman who raised you? What was she like?" Jennifer asked. She tore open a fluffy croissant, allowing flecks of it to flash across the table.

Heather allowed herself to picture Jane's face once more—hovering over her as she whispered, "Sweet dreams," every night before her untimely death.

"She was kind, gentle, and so loving," Heather whispered. "Everything I hope my daughters could say about me."

"Then Adam did the right thing," Kim said softly. "He knew where the love was. And he took you there. I only wish… I only wish I would have known. I would have taken you in as my own."

Heather's eyes brimmed with tears as she tried to regain control. Kim left for a moment, then returned with a large photo album, which she splayed open on the table. The first page held a very old photograph of a couple of eighteen-year-old kids—Heather's grandparents and Kim and Melanie's parents, who'd been married in 1951, a year before Kim's birth. Heather's grandmother, Greta, wore a very simple white dress with a high neckline and carried a small bouquet of flowers, which Kim said she'd hand-selected herself from her own mother's garden. Her grandfather, Hank, gazed at Greta as though she was the single-greatest answer to life's biggest mysteries.

"They died when I was twenty and Melanie was eighteen," Kim explained. "Awful car accident. Melanie was at cheerleading practice when it happened."

Silence fell over them. Kim flicked through the pages to find later photographs, ones of Melanie as a teenager in her cheerleading uniform. Heather's heart stung. Melanie seemed identical to her as a teenager; some of the photos echoed Kristine and Bella's faces, as well. In the sixties, Melanie seemed bright, iconic, assured and genuinely in love with whoever held the camera. In her youth, by contrast, Heather had been incredibly shy and had frequently hidden herself away when a camera had appeared. Despite that, she had been popular, more so than Casey and Nicole had ever been. Maybe whatever Melanie had, she'd taken along with her.

"Who was this person?" Heather whispered to the photograph.

Jennifer collected Oliver to put him down for a nap. Kim studied her hands as she prepared to answer.

"I want to tell you something good about her. Nothing obliterates all she did to you and to Adam and to everyone she knew later in life. Nothing obliterates how much she broke my heart, too," Kim continued. "But if there's one thing I remember, it's this. She loved our daddy, and he loved her, too. They had a very special relationship. He made her a little figurine of a horse out of wood. He whittled that thing every night on the porch. She loved that figurine to pieces. When they passed away, Melanie wept every night for weeks. I had to be strong for the both of us. And one of the last times I ever visited her where she was living, I saw that little horse. Proof that in some ways, she never really forgot that love." She paused briefly.

"There's no knowing what went through Melanie's mind when she left you with Adam, but I want to believe there was some good left in Melanie— something to cling to. So I'll say this. She probably saw the love Adam had for you. It was as real and as bright as anything else and probably a whole lot stronger than what she could offer. Maybe it reminded her of the way our daddy had loved her. Maybe she wanted you to have that."

Kim shook her head. Outside, thunder rolled across the mountains. She wiped aside a tear as Heather tried her best to suppress a sob.

"I have to hope that she wanted to do her best in some way," Kim continued. "Because she was my sister, and I did love her. I did. I have spent every year since 1999 regretting that I didn't reach out to her in some way. And now, you're here, Heather. You're here, and you've brought a hundred ghosts along with you. I don't know what to say except that if you and I could be friends— if we could find a way through this together, then maybe I will find a way to be all right. And maybe I can help you be all right, too."

Heather sat in Luke's truck an hour later. Her stomach growled with hunger. Luke revved the engine and dropped his head back against the seat. They hadn't managed to say a word since their goodbyes to Kim and Jennifer and Oliver.

Heather turned her head and found Luke's eyes. She could have fallen into those eyes, wrapped herself in the brilliant, yet comfortable greys, felt the enormity of the emotion behind his face. Instead, she gripped his hand and said, "Thank you for bringing me here today. I don't know if I feel better, exactly. But I feel closer to something."

"Maybe that's all it can be," Luke told her. "A search for meaning in a cruel universe."

Heather laughed. She wanted to kiss him, but she held herself back. She was an emotional goop.

"The love they have between one another reminded me of my

own life. Of Aunt Tracy and Jane, of Casey and Nicole. Of my life with Kristine and Bella," Heather whispered. "It reminded me of all I have. And how I want to hold tight to everything and keep it close. I want to love better than I have ever before."

"I have a pretty sincere doubt Jennifer and Kim will let you go now that they have found you," Luke said. "Imagine getting the likes of a successful, beautiful writer in the family suddenly. It's like winning the lottery."

Luke drove them back toward the Keating Inn. Heather felt rattled, weak. She wanted to fall into Nicole's arms and tell her everything.

"We'll find your family someday soon, Luke," Heather promised him again. "But in the meantime, I hope you know I have your back in every way."

Luke nodded. "Ditto."

CHAPTER TWENTY-THREE

A FAMILIAR VEHICLE sat outside of the Keating House. Heather pressed her hands over her heart at the sight. "I can't believe she came," she whispered.

"Who?"

But Heather flung herself out of the truck before she could answer. She rushed through the now-torrential rain and ran up the steps to find Nicole and Casey seated on the porch swing, both of them blotchy-cheeked with red-tinged eyes. From where Heather stood, Casey and Nicole could have been twins, with their similarities in features. They were the children of Jane Harvey and Adam Keating. Heather, on the other hand, was not.

"HEATHER!" Casey bolted to her feet and rushed toward her. In an instant, she flung her arms around Heather. Nicole joined them, and the weight of her impact nearly toppled them all to the floor.

Heather drew her face back and beamed up at her older sister.

Within her eyes, she saw a million memories reflected: a teenaged Casey who'd held Heather in the wake of her first breakup; a twenty-something Casey who'd insisted Heather stop messing around with other projects when all she really wanted to do was be a writer; a forty-something Casey who'd made space for Heather in her bed for those first few nights after Max's accident— when just the weight of another human body in bed beside her was enough to allow her a few hours of sleep.

"Heather, me and Nicole should kill you for running off like that," Casey growled, ever the older sister.

Heather's chin quivered. "I'm so sorry, Nic." She gripped her other sister's elbow and found her eyes. "There's no excuse for taking off like that." She then lifted her eyes to Casey as a slow smile crept toward her ear. "And you. I thought you said you'd never come to Bar Harbor. Not in your life."

"Yeah? Well, we all said that, and look at us now," Casey said as she flared her nostrils. "I guess the Harvey sisters aren't so trustworthy after all."

"We get it from our parents," Nicole affirmed.

Down below, Luke rolled down the window of his truck and waved a hand. Heather's heart shot toward him. She lifted her own arm out from the protection of the porch as she called, "Thank you for today." He knew, intuitively, that she needed this time with Nicole and Casey. There was so much she never had to say aloud to him.

She returned her gaze to her sisters. Nicole stepped into the foyer to fetch a bottle of wine and instructed the other two to head around to the outdoor table, where they could drink and talk and watch the boats pass by. Heather's tongue felt terribly heavy; she wasn't sure how she could explain this story all over again.

With Nicole inside, Heather and Casey sat across from one another at the outdoor table. Casey wrapped herself in a zip-up hoodie and crossed her arms tight. Her eyes squinted slightly as she studied Heather ominously.

"What?" Heather finally blurted. Within her voice, she heard her teenage self— purposefully arguing with her older sister.

"I told you not to come to Bar Harbor," she said.

"Yeah? Well, that ship's sailed," Heather returned.

Silence fell. Inside, there was the clacking sound of Nicole as she grabbed the wine glasses from the rack. It suddenly felt like ages since Heather had seen Casey. She'd hardly asked Casey how she was— often all alone in that big house these days since her own kids had left the nest and her husband, Grant, traveled so frequently for work.

Heather gripped Casey's hand over the table. Casey's eyes glistened with tears.

"You know, all I could think the past year was about your mental health," Casey said finally. "So often, when I looked in your eyes, I felt this distance between us. Like, with Max gone, you lost something of yourself that we could never get back."

Heather wasn't sure what to say. She'd felt far away, too, as though the devastation had tugged her so far from reality and from her sisters that she would never return.

"But I see you here," Casey breathed. "You're back. This is the Heather I've missed. I don't know how I know it. But there's something in your eyes. Something that tells me everything is going to be all right."

Heather's lower lip quivered. Nicole entered the porch, the wine glasses glistening. Deep in the distance, over the horizon of the wild ocean, a lightning bolt shattered through the darkness. Thunder followed shortly after.

"Remember what Mom always did when there was a storm?" Nicole asked. She propped up the glasses and placed the point of the wine opened gently in the center of the cork.

"How could I forget?" Casey asked with a smile. "Heather, you were particularly smitten with this."

Heather tilted her head. She drove through her memories, struggling to find the image. "I don't really remember."

Nicole and Casey exchanged a glance.

"You were young when she died. Maybe too young to fully remember," Nicole said. She performed a final thrust and removed the cork from the bottle. "Basically, when it first started to rain, Mom would get us girls all together and run out into the yard. We would always dance and sing until we were drenched or until the lightning got too close, or both. Then, we would hover on that porch we had in Portland, remember it? And we would count the seconds between thunder and lightning."

Heather's eyes filled with tears. She could only half-remember it— her clothes clinging to her like a second skin, her voice wild and loud and rocketing through the sky as she sang along with her sisters and mother.

"She could be wild when she wanted to be," Nicole affirmed.

Heather dropped her chin. "It's so strange to me that she wasn't my biological mother. I mean, even during those moments, she must have looked down at me— at my jet-black hair and blue eyes and second-guessed everything."

Nicole and Casey looked at her.

"I don't think she second-guessed anything. Not for a second," Casey affirmed.

"Mom loved you," Nicole insisted. "I remember I was so jealous of you when we were kids. I always thought you got more of everything."

"You were Mom's baby," Casey said with a laugh. "More candy. More playtime. More toys."

Heather burst into laughter. "You're kidding. That can't be true."

"Oh, but it is," Casey affirmed. "I remember it well. And Mom used to stay up late with you, making up little stories."

Heather chewed at her lower lip. She could only remember lit bits of it, how her mother would make up these little voices for some of her dolls as they worked through whatever fantasy land they'd invented. "We must save the princess!" Jane had cried, operating a little toy soldier. In this story, if Heather remembered correctly, she was the princess. "My little princess."

Heather closed her eyes and lifted her glass of wine. "I have so much to tell you both. But right now, I want to give a toast to Adam Keating and, even more than that, Jane Harvey. They were my parents. They loved me enough to help me make it through. And they gave me the two of you— women I trust, women I believe in, women I love more than I even know how to express."

Casey and Nicole lifted their glasses. In unison, the three of them said, "To Jane and to Adam. We love you, forever."

It took Heather another full hour to describe everything she'd learned. Nicole and Casey were dutiful listeners. They'd had many hours of practice, after all, throughout Heather's youth, when she'd returned from school with a tale of a horrible boy or a bad, unfair grade. They asked questions when needed but mostly allowed Heather to come all the way to the end. Here, she lifted her phone to show the photograph of her birth certificate, along with a photo she'd taken of her grandparents, Greta and Hank Hyde.

"Look at them," Casey breathed, taking the phone in her hands. "They're perfect."

"It was remarkable when Kim opened the door," Heather said softly. "I looked at her and I swear, I saw my face, the way it will look in twenty-five years. It was eerie. She knew something was up when she looked at me, too. She said it was like seeing a ghost."

"This Melanie woman," Nicole said, her brow furrowed. "She doesn't sound anything like you."

Heather bit her lower lip. "I was worried about that. That somehow, I'd taken on some of her negative characteristics. I'd always thought this depression that I can't escape came from Adam. But maybe, maybe it was her."

"Or maybe, you're a case of nurture versus nature," Nicole said. "And your depression was actually a result of some pretty messed up stuff that happened to you." She gripped Heather's hand over the table and gave her a subtle, genuine smile. "Melanie was cruel and manipulative. Some children are unlucky enough to live with cruel and manipulative mothers. You were lucky enough to escape that."

"We lived in a beautiful clubhouse together," Casey said. "The three Harvey girls and our beautiful mother. And when she passed on, we got Aunt Tracy. It's like our luck was never-ending."

"For a while," Nicole pointed out.

"Yes, well. We all have to grow up sometimes, don't we?" Casey murmured.

"I suppose we do," Heather breathed.

"Although you spend all your days in storybooks," Casey stated. "Writing them and reading them."

"I tried to escape reality as long as I could," Heather said. "But it caught up to me, I'm afraid."

"You should write about us," Nicole said. "About the three Harvey sisters and their mother and their home in the sky. About how they danced in the rain and sang silly songs. How it didn't matter they weren't all related— that they had enough love to pass around."

Heather began the song a few minutes later. She stood from her chair and wandered off the porch, where the first gashes of a brand-new rain came over her. As she lifted her chin, she began to sing.

"I come home in the morning' light; my mother says, 'When you gonna live your life right?'"

And then, Casey and Nicole rushed from the porch and into the rain after her, calling out the lyrics to their long-forgotten favorite eighties tune. They danced and twirled as they cried out, "Oh momma dear, we're not the fortunate ones, and girls, they wanna have fun!"

Now, Heather could remember them singing this exact song, maybe only a year before Jane passed away, drenched down to their skin, swinging their arms toward the sky. When they finished all the words they remembered, they fell back on the porch stairs, wiping their cheeks of both tears and rain.

"I really convinced myself for a moment it was actually 1983," Casey said softly.

"Me too," Nicole replied.

They held the silence for a moment. Heather's heart felt too big for her ribcage. When she lifted her chin, another razor-sharp lightning bolt shattered through the sky.

"I have this feeling that we're missing pieces of ourselves," she said finally. "Right here, in Dad's old place. I think we should bring all our kids here before the weather fully breaks for winter. I want Bella and Kristine to know the truth. And I want us all together here, under this roof. We are building new memories. Finding new ways to love each other. Okay?"

"Okay," Nicole agreed. "But I think we should invite everyone for dinner. Really everyone."

"What do you mean?" Heather asked.

Casey arched an eyebrow. "You know, your new Aunt Kim and your new cousins, along with that adorable toddler, Oliver?"

Heather's laughter was like music. "You think they'll really want to come?"

"Only one way to find out," Nicole said.

"And who wouldn't want you as family?" Casey demanded. "You're trying to get out of the Harvey circle, and me and Nicole are doing everything in our power to keep you in it. You're ours for good. You hear?"

"Loud and clear," Heather affirmed.

CHAPTER TWENTY-FOUR

IT WAS PERHAPS the last beautiful day of the year. An eggshell blue sky warped overhead, like the crisp top of a perfect snow globe — one that, from overhead, showed a picaresque little New England town on the coast of Frenchman Bay, tucked there against the Acadia Mountains on the island of Mount Desert. Heather lifted her chin and watched as an airplane drew a sputtering line through the blue, her hand extended over her stomach. Although she'd lost the baby weight quite quickly, she'd never fully gotten rid of the saggy skin in the wake of her twins. She could feel it now, beneath the weight of her dress's fabric. Did Melanie have similar skin after she'd given birth to her? What had she thought when she'd held baby Heather in her arms?

Heather reminded herself, now, that Melanie hadn't even bothered to come up with a name beyond her own— that her name had come from Adam, instead. Some mothers just weren't cut it out to love well. Some mothers just couldn't mother.

From the porch, there came again the rollicking, vibrant sound of Oliver laughing as Kristine and Bella tossed him back and forth between them. Heather had already half-scolded them to take care, to play safe, but Oliver kept insisting on silly, rough play. At this, Jennifer, her cousin, had just grumbled and said, "Just wear him out. He needs a nap soon."

Heather turned and took in the full view of her family, who were stationed out across the porch, eating barbecue and drinking wine and beer and bantering. Jennifer's brother, Jeremy, had brought his entire family by, and one of his sons was the same age as Kristine and Bella, which had thrown them into an argument about some newly-released movie and how good it was.

"They're already fighting like family," Jeremy had laughed as he'd hugged Heather close. "Welcome. No matter how long it took you to join us, I want to welcome you."

Luke appeared on the top of the staircase. He wore a light grey collared shirt and a pair of dark jeans. Somehow, his grey eyes made the lush green of the surrounding trees and the thick grass beneath Heather glow even more. She remembered a week before after she and Casey, and Nicole had finished their dance in the rain. She'd told them that she'd never envisioned herself falling in love again. "Max was it for me. And then, I met Luke."

Nicole and Casey pestered her for details. All she would tell them was that she wasn't yet ready but that maybe, if he kept up his ridiculous patience, she would be, soon.

"Maybe this is the universe telling me something— that I shouldn't dwell in the sorrows of the past. That I will always love Max, but I can make room for other experiences, too. Maybe it's telling me to drop all my anger and resentment and move forward."

Luke came toward her. Heather's tongue dried up with fear. She tried to play it cool, like a teenager on the brink of collapse.

"Thanks for coming to our silly family barbecue," Heather said.

"Silly? I would have killed for something like this back in the day," Luke said. "I soak up as many family get-togethers as I can."

Heather smiled. She lifted her chin, so yearning again to kiss him. She held herself back and instead brushed her fingers against his.

"I heard a rumor you're thinking about staying," Luke said then.

"It's a rumor," Heather said. "But it's mostly about my dart game. See, I beat you. But I still plan on beating every other person in Bar Harbor."

"Ah. So you're staying for competition's sake," he said.

"Something like that."

Luke's smile was crooked and spectacularly cute. "Well, I'd like it if you found it within yourself to call me, even though you've found a way through your problems."

"Naw. I'm pretty selfish," Heather said. "Now that I've used you for all you're worth, I won't need you anymore. Maybe we'll see each other from time to time, but that's about it."

"Fair enough," Luke replied. "Thanks for being honest with me."

"Yeah. It's kind of my policy," Heather told him.

They held one another's gaze for a moment. Heather's heart performed a backflip. She realized suddenly that she hadn't gone searching for Max's box of cigarettes in many days. It would always remain there for her, a direct link to her past.

But it was up to her to build her future.

"Heather! Get up here!" Nicole called from up on the porch, where she stood with a wine glass balanced between two fingers and a plate of barbecue fish tacos.

"I'm being called," Heather said playfully to Luke.

"Guess you'd better get up there then."

Heather hustled up the stairs to find Kristine, Bella, and baby Oliver on the creaking porch swing. Uncle Joe's daughter, Brittany, hovered behind while Casey and Nicole's children gathered around.

"We want to take a photo," Nicole said.

"We're a modern American family," Casey affirmed.

"Come on, Mom," Kristine said as she padded a hand across the spare bit of porch swing. "You brought us all together. You deserve center stage."

Heather weaved her way between her twin girls, both of whom seemed to sizzle with personality they'd gotten from their father. Luke suggested that he take the photo, but that was soon dismissed, as Nicole insisted he get in the photo, too. Eventually, they set up a timer on the phone— an act that resulted in them having to take the same photograph several times. On the last one, Kristine and Bella cried, "A silly one!" and everyone made funny faces, then burst into laughter.

When Heather looked at the photos later that evening, with both Kristine and Bella's heads on opposite shoulders, her heart felt fuller than it had in the year since Max's passing. When she'd first told Nicole she would come to Bar Harbor to help out around the Keating Inn and Acadia Eatery, she couldn't have envisioned the different path she would eventually take.

Yet here was that path. And here was the rest of her life. There, across the rocky coastline of Bar Harbor, a place where her father—a man who'd loved hard and lost everything, had known how to set her on a path of unlimited love.

"Thank you, Adam," she breathed now as she lifted her eyes toward Cadillac Mountain. "I know you're here with us, too."

OTHER BOOKS BY KATIE

The Vineyard Sunset Series

Secrets of Mackinac Island Series

Sisters of Edgartown Series

A Katama Bay Series

Made in the USA
Las Vegas, NV
06 November 2021